THE LOST NECKLACE

SHAIVA PANDYA

ISBN 979-8-89322-955-4

To My Beloved Mom,
Who Sacrificed Her Dreams So That Mine Could Soar!

Acknowledgement

So, here I am, turning two as an author! Why did I start writing this? Beats me. Why did I start writing anything in the first place? I might have a clue. My mom once told me that she always knew I was going to do something in the realm of art with my writing skills. I raised an eyebrow sceptically and asked, 'How did you figure that out?' She said, 'Well, kiddo, when you were young, you used to pen letters to God, hoping for some divine wisdom to sort out your existential crises. I figured if you could eloquently write to the Big Guy then, you would only get better with time.'

Her words stuck a chord. I got into all kinds of letter writing, love letters, break-up letters, job application letters, resignation letters, letters to myself (originally intended for God, but redirected to myself due to the mysterious and elusive mailing address of the Almighty). Naturally, I never heard back from the divine mailbox and my attempts at explaining my innermost thoughts fell flat. So, I ditched letter writing and picked up novel writing to seek answers to life's big questions.

Just kidding!

My novels are not philosophical, or at least not yet! With "The Lost Necklace" I'm here to provide three things: Entertainment, Pure Entertainment, and Yup, you guessed it right, Absolute Entertainment that you can consume with a tub full of cheese popcorn.

Now, onto the acknowledgements.

I would like to thank my dearest mom for saving up all those letters, essays, and stories that I wrote as a child and giving me the confidence to turn my passion into a profession. A heartfelt shoutout to my dad for genetically transferring his excellent linguistic and writing skills. He always said (or probably borrowed it from someone wise) One can only succeed in their endeavour if they act to express and not to impress. So, here I am expressing the journey I took with the complex and intricate characters of this story in my mind. Will you be impressed? Only time will tell or probably reviews on Amazon. Ah, the modern age!

I've gotta give a shoutout to Karan Kapasi for being a partner in plot-twisting crime. From hashing out storylines to brainstorming absurd endings, we've taken Firdaus and Aryan (the dynamic duo of this tale) on a wild journey. Also, a big hug to Parth Joshi for crafting an eye-catching cover art- what a stunner, seriously! Last but not the least, many thanks to Vajirapani Hewabattage for transforming my jumble of A4 pages into a polished masterpiece. You're a magician with a keyboard!

I would also like to thank all my friends and family for supporting me through this journey. You all have been my biggest cheerleaders. Everyone who read and reviewed the initial draft of this story, a big thank you and lots of love.

Now, let me share a bit about the ideation of the plotline.

I've long been captivated by action-adventure thrillers such as Dan Brown's gripping tales like The Da Vinci Code and Angels & Demons, as well as Steve Berry's compelling work like The Alexandria Link. My guilty pleasures also include repeatedly indulging in globe-trotting treasure hunt movies like The Mummy series, the iconic Bond 007 franchise, and the adventurous escapades of The National Treasure. And of course, the list wouldn't be complete without mentioning the timeless allure of Indiana Jones. The inception of "The Lost Necklace" occurred during my viewing of a TV series of a similar genre, sparking the idea to craft a tale that delivers pure entertainment. I aspired to weave a narrative brimming with adventure, thrill, action, and emotions, all interwoven into an extraordinary saga centred around lost Indian treasures. Throughout history, Indian royals possessed countless unique jewels and treasures, many of which were lost during independence movements or pilfered due to corruption. "The Lost Necklace" delves into one of these precious artifacts, the renowned Patiala Necklace. While the story incorporates elements of history entwined with myths and folklore, it is important to note that it remains a work of fiction. It does not seek to alter, distort, or manipulate any actual historical events. All the names, characters, businesses, places, events, and incidents depicted in this book stem from my imagination, influenced by stories I've encountered over time. Any resemblance to actual persons, living or deceased, or real events is purely coincidental.

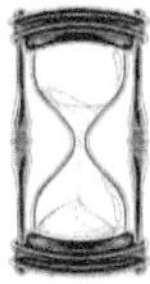

Chapter 1
New Delhi

Aryan Verma despised one thing above all — being late. He had low tolerance for tardiness and held an unwavering expectation of utmost punctuality from everyone, including himself. Yet, much to his annoyance, today was one of those days where time seemed to have had it out for him. Everything he did backfired as if the universe was working against him. The alarm accidentally snoozed, the milk on the stove overflowed before he could turn off the gas, hot water wasn't hot enough and his car keys decided to play hide and seek.

It was one of those days, when luck decides to take a day off and Murphy's Law evidently proves itself.

'Move out of my way!' he suddenly screamed. His father's old Honda City was about to crash into a motor scooter that had slithered into the spot between his car and the car ahead of him. He pressed the horn hard and scowled at the driver ahead of him. 'Can't you drive properly?' he yelled. The guy on the scooter turned around and gave him a death stare as if he would get off his two-wheeler and punch his face if he dared to speak another word.

'Delhi traffic is the worst; I should have taken the Metro.' He muttered, but slightly louder than usual. The guy before him turned again and glared at him through his helmet. 'I am talking to myself; do you have a problem with that too?' The thin man with an oversized leather jacket turned his head again and yelled a few curse words. Although Aryan mainly was a peaceful person, he was easy to instigate. He got out of his car to smack a punch on the thin guy's pale jaws, but the traffic light turned green as he walked towards the scooter, and the guy rode off before Aryan could reach him. As the honking around him turned louder, Aryan rushed back to his car. 'Bloody moron,' he cursed, pulling up his window.

Right outside his office, he found himself stuck in a traffic jam caused by a rickshaw driver who had chosen to pick up a passenger from the wrong side of the road. Aryan grimaced for a second and then realized it was pointless complaining. He had to find a way to reach work on time. He dropped his window glass again and whistled to grab the watchman's attention. The man in the grey uniform guarding the main gate of a massive colonial building quickly whisked his way through the traffic and reached the spot where Aryan was stuck. Aryan got off the vehicle and handed him the key.

'Lakshman, please park the car and be cautious. Don't scratch it.' He yelled with his head towards the gate.

'Ji, Sir!' The watchman replied, getting into the car.

'Why are you late?' A voice came from the tea stall located on the side of the building. Aryan saw a few of his colleagues waving at him.

'I am late for a meeting. I'll see you guys later!' He screamed, waving back.

Aryan never truly enjoyed working as an Administrative Officer at the Archaeological Survey of India. He knew he could do more with his many talents but was always too scared to try. He was sharp, intuitive, and loyal towards his job. He hated not coming on time and passing the day pretending to work, even though his colleagues would do that without an inch of regret.

He ran up the stairs frantically, hoping to make it to the meeting that had popped on his calendar just an hour before.

Ram, his manager at ASI, pulled up his hand and waved at him from a distance, 'Good morning, Aryan.'

'Good morning, sir!' Aryan replied with a sigh of relief, knowing he finally got in on time, at least before the boss.

Ram pushed the door and allowed Aryan to walk into the room. 'Aryan, I would like you to meet Ms Firdaus Durrani.' A strikingly beautiful woman was sitting on the chair next to the conference table. Firdaus looked charming and radiant. She wore black trousers and a loose white blouse, an attire usually suitable for corporate meetings. Her dark brown hair was neatly swept up and tied atop her head. One look at her was enough for Aryan to bring back all the memories he had conveniently stashed in the corner of his heart.

The hatred he had fought so hard to bury had been summoned. His past had resurfaced, and with it came the memories that hurt every fibre of his body. The woman he once loved was now back in his life. All the events that made Aryan skim through his horoscope in the morning, finally made sense. With a flustered face, he said, 'Firdaus Durrani, to what do I owe this displeasure!' Ram was taken aback by Aryan's greetings. He had never seen him so brazen and daring. Aryan stood at the door feeling disgusted, looking at a woman who was otherwise known for her bewitching charm.

'I am sorry for my colleague's behaviour, Ms Durrani.' Ram apologized instantly and glared at Aryan hinting him to do the same.

Aryan realized that he had acted against his better judgment and had to apologize to the woman he hated so much, if he wanted to save his job. 'I am very sorry, Firdaus.' His face reflected no shame or regret but sheer resentment.

'It's alright! To be honest, I had never thought we would cross paths again.' She replied with equal asperity. The room fell silent as Firdaus took a moment to let her apprehension sink in. Watching Aryan walk through the door, she knew her fate was sealed.

Trying to break the uncalled-for silence and awkwardness, Ram cleared his throat loudly and said, 'Aryan, Ms Durrani has come to us with a proposal. She needs our help, and we're here to support her. Is that clear?' He sounded authoritative.

Firdaus interrupted immediately, 'Ram! If Mr Verma is not comfortable with my presence, he is free to leave. I am sure your department has other capable individuals willing to work with me.'

'There won't be a need for that. Aryan is a good employee, and, importantly, he is determined, something you wanted from our man. He is the right person for this job. I assure you of that.' Ram drifted his gaze from Firdaus to Aryan. His stare was unnerving. 'Aryan, do you have any problem working with Ms Durrani?'

'No, Sir!' he replied.

Firdaus couldn't stop herself from sneering. 'Ah, classic Aryan, too scared to say no?' She thought.

'Very well then.' Moving her mind to the task, she clicked the red button on the remote and switched on the audio-visual system. A black and white picture of the late Prince of Patiala was displayed on the screen. Firdaus zoomed in to show the necklace in the image.

'This is Prince Amrendra Singh of Patiala, and the gorgeous necklace you see was his most treasured jewel, known to the world as the Patiala Necklace!' Aryan and Ram's eyes sparkled as their attention turned to the grandiosity and opulence of the Necklace.

'This masterpiece is studded with 234 Carat yellow octahedral De Beers diamond found in the De Beers mines in the late 19th century. It includes five rows of platinum chains encrusted with 2930 diamonds, some Burmese rubies, and a centrepiece diamond, the size of a golf ball.'

Firdaus changed the picture, and an image of the royal family of Patiala with the British viceroy and his family flashed on the screen. 'The tall man in this picture is Prince Amrendra Singh's father, Maharaj Rajinder Singh. On the left is his wife, his two daughters and the little prince, and on the right is the 10th Viceroy of India, Lord Wellington, followed by his wife, Elizabeth Wellington and daughter, Emily Wellington. Rumour has it that Ms Emily and Maharaja Rajinder Singh were in love.

Their clandestine affair had not only broken hearts but provoked riots and chaos across the state. Threats were made to end their romance, and bribes were offered to silence the gossip, but soon the news spread like wildfire and a major revolt from both sides followed consequently.

She changed the image and showed a rustic newspaper clipping on the screen. 'This report narrates the story of the night that changed history.' She looked at Aryan and Ram to make sure she had their attention. When she saw their eyes glued to hers, she narrated the story.

'In 1894, Emily was exiled and ordered to return to London. Her father's command was against her wish, so one night, she took the carriage and went to the palace to meet the king. She begged the king to run off with her. He was stunned by her courage, and if it wasn't for Duty, he would have run off with her. His enslaved heart urged him to give in to her wishes, but his crown propelled him to do otherwise. As a token of his love for her, he gave Emily his necklace, the family heirloom and the first and original Patiala necklace. He asked her to make a journey to Kolkata. Soon after her departure, he informed the Imperial army of her whereabouts. His betrayal led the militia to Emily, who was then taken to the port of Surat for immediate departure. That night, a mob broke out at the dock as the locals received a tip that the British ships were about to sail with the looted treasure. The flared violence left Emily with no choice but to run for her life. She stuffed the necklace into her bra and ran towards the road to call for help. She used the Patiala necklace to get her a ride to the south. She offered to give the Necklace to the person who showed willingness to help her. She was immediately taken aboard on a bullock cart by a few local villagers who would have done anything for a dime.'

Firdaus again looked around to make sure that everyone in the room had their attention. She had nothing to worry about. No one moved or fidgeted or looked anywhere else but her. The room was still and both Ram and Aryan looked focused.

'You might be wondering, why am I narrating this rigmarole tale of a doomed love?' She looked at the boys again. 'The short answer is that Maharaja Rajinder Singh's Necklace, also known as the original Patiala Necklace, made its way back to the Patiala Treasury in the early 1900s. It was then reconstructed by Cartier for the prince in 1928. And then, it disappeared in 1948 and has not been found to date. The hundred-million-dollar necklace is lost or stolen. Who knows?' She paused briefly and then continued, 'Pronounced cursed and doomed, the Patiala necklace was a proof of betrayal for the Maharaja and pure decadence for his prince.'

'By now, I am sure we know what we're looking for. Is that right?' She asked.

Aryan nodded.

'The Royal International Art & Antiquity Exhibition is happening in London in 10 days, and we must find this necklace before that to exhibit the pride of India', Firdaus continued.

Aryan took his eyes off her and looked at Ram. 'Sir, what do you want me to do? Am I to accompany Ms Durrani in her quest for the necklace? Is that what ASI wants?' His voice was sharp, and his posture confident.

'Yes, Aryan. Not just for the ASI but for the nation!' exclaimed Ram. 'We need to find the necklace!'

The tea stall was now scarcely crowded; only the man who owned the stall and a random fellow who looked aimless stuck around. The ASI employees had returned to their bleak desks and mundane tasks, and the others waiting for the traffic to clear had returned to the road. Aryan ordered two cups of tea and patiently waited for the man to prepare it. Aryan took out his phone and checked the messages that had popped up during the meeting. When he found nothing important, he threw the phone back into his pocket.

Firdaus sat silently on one of the benches next to the tea stall. Engrossed in her thoughts, she marvelled through the fears and inhibitions that came along with Aryan. The chaos of her thoughts subdued the cacophony of the buzzing horns that came from the road. As her thoughts swung between the past and the present, she didn't listen to Aryan when he called her.

'Here is your tea, the way you like it.' Aryan offered the cup to Firdaus.

'Firdaus, your tea!' Aryan snapped his fingers in front of her face to grab her attention.

'Sorry, I was lost in my thoughts.' She blew into the cup a couple of times before taking her first sip. The tea had less milk and more cardamom, which was exactly the way she liked it. 'You still remember how I take my tea?' She asked in surprise.

'Yes, I do. I remember a lot of things, Firdaus.' She saw Aryan's face reddening as he stared at her with resentment.

'I trusted you, and you betrayed me.'

Firdaus rolled her eyes at his blame. 'You know nothing.' Her eyes depended as she pondered her past. 'Well, it doesn't matter anymore. I don't want to discuss our past. Let us try to keep our feelings, be it hate or love, to ourselves.' Will that work for you?

'LOVE and that too for you. I would rather go to hell'. He mumbled, followed by a scornful smirk.

'Finding the Patiala Necklace is important to both of us. Especially you, if you want to keep your job.'

'I know you well enough to assume that you're more than capable of finding the Patiala Necklace yourself, so why come to ASI? His question made her nervous. 'What do you mean?' she stuttered. 'You got the wrong idea; it is the ASI who hired me for this hunt.' Oh, Firdaus, save your lies for someone else.' She looked straight into his eyes. 'I am not lying.' She said in her defence. 'So, are you telling me that the moment you get your hands on that stupid necklace, you'll not steal it and run away?' 'Okay, that's it! I will not explain myself to you anymore. If you want to come, you're welcome to join and if you don't want to come, please go back and tell that to your boss.'

Firdaus threw her empty cup into the dustbin and made her way to the main gate. 'Stop.' Aryan yelled from behind. 'I'll come with you.' He brisked his way to her. 'Tell me what you have in mind.'

'I don't have a plan, but I know where to start. Five years ago, Dr. Pearl DeMello wrote a book called Filthy Rich Royals. When researching, she extensively studied the life of Prince Amrendra Singh and his family. She is in Goa right now; we can meet her and see what she has to say about the Patiala Necklace.'

'Alright, lead the way.' He sighed.

'You don't want to go with me?'

'How does it matter? Do I have a choice? I need this job and to keep it, I must come with you.'

'Aryan, I don't want to fight, and I don't have the strength for this mindless bickering.'

'I don't want to fight either, but I can't stop myself.' Firdaus stared at him but didn't respond. 'A few seconds later, Aryan apologised. 'Fine, I am sorry. Let's go to Goa.'

Chapter 2
Abu Dhabi

Mukhtar Rahman, a.k.a Debojeet Bagchi, arrived at the Abu Dhabi airport in his private jet. Rahman's father was one of the Mukti Bahinis. They fought gallantly against the Pakistani army during the Bangladesh Liberation War in 1971. After his death in 1972, the five-year-old Mukhtar came to India and changed his name to Debojeet Bagchi. Born into a Muslim family in Bangladesh, Bagchi posed as a Hindu, a Bengali to be precise, almost all his life. At an early age, he understood nothing was more fulfilling than being rich and powerful. The self-taught Bangladeshi kid tricked some powerful people into his nefarious schemes. He used them to build his network. Somehow, he also succeeded in scheming the rich for their money and sent them to jail by siding with the police. With the acquired money, he built a business empire that made him the Copper King of India.

Debojeet Bagchi got off the plane with a four-year-old girl and her babysitter. A finely dressed lady received them at the tarmac and escorted them to the spot where a shiny black limousine awaited their arrival. The little one clasped her teddy bear close to her chest and fixated her gaze upon the finely dressed woman who escorted them. The woman looked back with a warm smile. She extended both her hands, turned them into fists and asked the little one to pick one.

The child hesitated; her innocent eyes looked at her babysitter, seeking her permission. The babysitter gently patted her shoulder and said, 'Go ahead, my child. Pick one.' The girl pointed her finger, and the lady gave her the chocolate she had hidden in her fist.

'What is your name?' She Asked.

'Ariana,' the girl replied in a low and nervous voice.

'Your granddaughter is beautiful,' Mr Bagchi.

'Thank you!' He replied, keeping his conversation succinct.

The woman was arrested by the look he gave, captivated by something in his aura. Beneath Bagchi's unforgettable charm and captivating voice, lurked a Mephistopheles-like presence. His personality was so compelling that anyone who stood beside him or engaged in conversation couldn't easily shake him from their thoughts, unless he willed it otherwise.

He gestured to Ariana to get into the car. Even the little one could not resist his command, she jumped into the car straight away and settled in the corner seat. Bagchi sat next to her and took out his phone to make a call. 'We are on our way!' He sounded ominous. He hung up and smiled at Ariana. The kid was too scared to smile; she looked away from him and hugged the teddy she was carrying.

The driver looked at him through the rearview mirror, 'Sir, Shangri La?' He asked.

'Yes, please.' The voice came from behind, and the car slowly pulled away from the curb and joined the traffic on the main road.

* * *

Mr. Charles Brown, the director of the International Art & Antiquity Exhibition, flounced into Mr Khan's suite. 'What the hell have you done?' He furiously asked.

'Calm down, Mr Brown. Everything is under control. Trust me.' Karim Khan replied.

With a cigar in one hand and a glass of whisky in another, Khan sat calmly in his white sheikh gown exuding an aura of a tyrant.

'Trust you, seriously? Had I known you are on the wanted list, I would have never offered you the deal.' Charles walked through the room, fuming in rage. Karim Khan gulped his drink and then refilled his glass with Bourbon from the bar. 'Mr. Brown, I don't believe a gentleman of your stature would be naïve enough to offer millions of dollars to a man without checking his background.'

'What the hell do you mean?' Charles glared at him.

'You came to me with this proposal despite knowing who I was, and that is because you knew I would do the job for you.' He said placidly.

Charles gulped the shot of whisky and slammed the glass on the table. 'Relax, Mr Brown, everything is under control. Our man is handling this with the utmost discretion. He'll be here anytime now and give you an update on the progress himself.'

'I hope you're right. Finding the Patiala Necklace is very important for both of us. However, the repercussions of getting caught are far worse for you than for me. I hope you know that.'

A knock on the door interrupted their conversation. 'Ah, my friend is here!' Said Khan.

'Salam, my dearest.' Debojeet greeted his friend.

'Walekum assalam, khushamdeed! Please come in.'

Bagchi entered and introduced himself to the white freckled man grumpily sitting on the couch. 'Nice to meet you Mr. Brown.'

Charles looked at him, still in rage. 'Mr Khan says you have hired someone to find the necklace. Is that right?' He asked boorishly.

'They're on it as we speak,' Bagchi replied.

'You believe they'll find the necklace in ten days?'

'Rest assured, they surely will.' Bagchi looked as calm and unperturbed as Khan.

Debojeet got up and motioned towards the window to catch some fresh air. Charles was still boiling with concerns. 'You speak too casually, Mr Bagchi. Have you thought of alternate outcomes? What if they don't find it? What if the government comes to know someone is looking for it? What if the necklace cease to exist or has been dismantled and destroyed?'

'Mr. Brown, you are too worried.' Khan replied. 'Have another glass of Whisky; it might take the edge off.'

'I don't concern myself with the improbability of its existence; I am sure it is there somewhere,' Bagchi shot back. 'It could be in India, or' he took a short pause, 'It could be in London, with other stolen treasure.'

'I don't like what you're insinuating. I would not be paying millions of dollars to you if the necklace was in England.' God forbid, if that's the case, I'll be the one bearing questions and scrutiny of the press, not you!'

'Well, my friend, you questioned our competence, and I returned the favour by questioning your integrity,' Bagchi retorted.

Bagchi was no fool to offend the man who was about to pay him a fortune. He was simply testing him. He wanted to make sure Charles knew what he was doing. Debojeet never underestimated anyone and nor did he trust them entirely. He would always do his due diligence before carrying out his next move.

'Trust is a two-way street, Mr Brown. If you don't trust us, we won't be able to trust you either.'

'Let us all relax and talk about the matter at hand.' Khan interfered. He admired Bagchi's confidence but feared that Charles might change his mind and take his business elsewhere, or worse cancel the deal altogether. So, he tried to shift the men's (particularly Charles's) attention to the hunt for Patiala's necklace.

'What do we know about this woman? Firdaus is her name, isn't it? Will she open her mouth?'

'She is good at her job. If there is anyone who can find this necklace, then that's her. As far as her allegiance is concerned, don't worry about it. She won't betray us.'

'Well, then, all is well. Mr Brown, I believe in my friend's words, and you should too.' Khan exhaled a sigh of relief.

Charles looked slightly relaxed. His furrowed brows were pulled apart and now rested in their normal position. 'I trust you guys to get the necklace for me in ten days. If you fail to do so, the deal is off the table. He solemnly waited for the men to nod in approval.

When Charles left, Bagchi settled in the living room with Khan to talk business. 'So, tell me what your real plan is?' Khan stared into Debojeet's eyes as he posed the question. His lips twitched into a smile. 'I love how you come straight to the point and never waste time.' Debojeet chuckled. 'I don't see a reason to prolong it when we both know why we are here.' 'I agree.' Karim nodded. 'I want to show you my dream. It is pure, almost heaven-like.' 'Then what are we waiting for? Let's go.

Bagchi's claustrophobia intensified as the men traversed the narrow tunnel. The stone wall got colder, and lanterns positioned at the entrance casted diminishing light as they ventured deeper. Bagchi's loud exhale caught Khan's attention. He turned around and said, 'I didn't know you were scared of closed spaces.' 'I am not scared, just a little uncomfortable.' 'Don't worry, just a few more steps and we'll be there.' Khan assured. Bagchi nodded and followed him through.

The tunnel opened into a large, more ventilated area which was brighter than the passageway. Debojeet and Karim entered the space and looked around. As the fire flickered in the cones hung on the rocky walls of the cave, the path further became more visible. Two uniformed men, who seemed like guards, welcomed the men into the facility.

Debojeet stopped to gasp for breath and calm his nerves. He looked around to mentally calculate how much deeper they had come beneath the ground. Drops of sweat circled his forehead as he breathed erratically. 'We are almost there.' Khan patted his shoulder and descended the ramp to the room of jewels. The precious jewels and artefacts of the world were laid out for display. Khan spared no moment before indulging in glorifying his victory. He opened his arms and said, '*Agar firdaus bar roo-e zameen ast, Hameen ast-o hameen ast-o hameen ast*' a Farsi couplet that literally translates as, if there is a paradise on earth, it is this, it is this, it is this. 'Mashallah', Bagchi spat out in surprise. 'This is just the gateway to heaven. I'll show you my paradise, and I bet you'll love it.' Karim pointed at an emerald studded curved dagger and said, 'you know what this is?' Bagchi nodded. 'This treasured Ottoman jewel was stolen from Topkapi palace in Istanbul and is worth millions of dollars in the black market.' A short laugh followed the statement. 'They still display a dagger that looks like this one to lure the tourists, but it's fake.' Karim pointed at an empty glass case next to the dagger and said, 'this one is for the Patiala Necklace.' The men exchanged a smile and moved to the vault adjacent to the jewel room.

Khan pushed some numbers on the lock and placed his thumb on the digital pad attached to it for biometric identification. Soon, the locks clicked, and the door opened. The vault's shelved walls displayed military weapons such as handguns and rifles that Karim claimed to have bought from ISIS. In the centre of the vault was a stand with a glass case that held a cylindrical structure that he referred to as his omen bearer.

Whether those were his words of hope or illusion, his omen bearer was a gateway to devastation. An atomic weapon that would take the lives of millions. Debojeet knew all about Khan's disturbing past, which became a lifelong saga of melancholy and later a cause for his vendetta. The moment he entered the vault he had known, Khan was planning something big, but when he saw the weapon, he realized that Khan's wish to avenge his family's death had taken over his sensibilities. His craving for revenge had blinded him of the consequences. In that instance, Bagchi promised to extend his support to Khan's cause, but he knew that Karim's myopic plan was only going to destroy them both.

Debojeet Bagchi came to the sobering realization that he had made a grave mistake by aligning himself with Khan. He had always known that his infatuation with wealth and power could ultimately lead to his downfall, but he hadn't anticipated that everything would unravel so swiftly. Accepting the deal solely for monetary gain would prove to be a fatal error that now threatened to consume him. He pondered, recognizing that if Khan's desires were to be fulfilled—God forbid—it wouldn't simply result in loss of lives, but would also unleash chaos upon the stock market, leading to losses from which his company would take forever to recover.

We are going to win this time. Khan announced. His arrogance was brutal, and he celebrated his victory even before going to war. A special celebratory arrangement was made for the men underground. A private viewing of belly dancing with free-flowing booze and sheesha. Bagchi forced a smile, 'my friend, don't you think we're celebrating too soon?' Khan took a slight offence at his friend's skepticism. 'Bagchi…. oh my dear Bagchi, why do you fear failing? Think of a morning when the sun will rise to the air filled with ashes of the dead. Ashes of the 'Kafirs.' 'Inshallah, it'll happen one day.' Bagchi held his friend's hand in assurance.

Chapter 3

Goa

Professor Pearl DeMello's bungalow in Panjim had the magnificence of Portuguese aesthetics combined with years of poor maintenance. An arched doorway led to a vast barren front yard, which was sadly derelict and desperately needed restoration.

'Seems Ms DeMello is not a fan of renovation,' Firdaus pointed out.

'But she is of gardening,' Aryan cocked his head, pointing his finger at the lush garden in the backyard.

Firdaus moved closer to the fence, peeking at the beautiful spread of green foliage. The astonishingly well-maintained garden exhibited Ms DeMello's peculiar interest in preserving one part of her property while the other fell apart, she thought.

'Ms DeMello, it's me, Firdaus; remember I spoke to you on the phone earlier? I am here to meet you.' She spoke loudly, trying to be audible to the lady standing at a far distance.

Pearl was watering her plants when she heard someone screaming through the fence. She pulled up her glasses and turned around. 'Missy, I am old, not deaf.' Her retort was sharp. Aryan smirked at her comment. 'What?' 'Nothing.' She gave him an acerbic look. Then she craned her neck through the fence and said, 'I am so sorry, Ms. DeMello.' This time, she kept her volume low.

'Do you have an appointment?' Pearl asked.

'Yes, I spoke to you on the phone. My colleague and I are here to talk about your book.'

'So, you're a journalist.'

'No, Ms DeMello, I am Mrs Mariam Durrani's daughter. You invited me to come and have a chat with you about your book. Remember?' 'Damn it, this senile lady will drive me crazy,' Firdaus whispered.

'Oh Firdaus, how are you, my child? Wait, let me open the front door.' She said, motioning to the door.

'Does Ms DeMello know your mother?' Aryan asked in surprise. 'Yes, she was my mother's professor.'

Pearl DeMello opened the door and welcomed them in. 'I now remember receiving a call from you. I am very sorry. I have a memory of a goldfish. Sometimes, I forget to eat lunch and starve all day, thinking I had it. You see, old age comes with its challenges.'

'That's fine, Ms DeMello. Happens to the best of us.'

'Oh darling, call me Pearl. Let me tell you, you're my favourite student's daughter. What a lovely kid your mother was! I heard of her passing, and it broke my heart. How did it happen? If you don't mind me asking?'

'It was an accident.'

'May God bless her soul. How are you doing now?'

'I am fine, Ms DeMello, I mean Pearl. Thanks for asking.'

'Come, have a seat.' The old lady moved the cushions on the couch to make room for the couple.

The interior of her house was in a pristine condition. The living room was adorned with a chandelier looking upon a magnificent leather sofa. The size of the room looked bigger than it really was because of the gorgeous parquetry flooring that spread across leading up until the back door that opened to the garden. Aryan gazed at the relics that were neatly displayed on the side table. Then he moved his eyes to the shelved library with copies of all sorts of literature. Although the living area was clean, the library was dusty and rustic.

She might be right; her memory is indeed unpredictable. Aryan wondered. Cleaning areas that are already clean and leaving the rest to decay is undoubtedly a sign of an unstable mind.

'So, what brings you here? What do you want to know? Pearl sat on the chair, primly across from Firdaus.

'The Patiala Necklace. We want to know where it is.' Firdaus replied.

'Oh, my dear, if it was that easy, many would have found it already.' Now, to answer your question, 'I don't know where it is.'

'Pearl, the thing is, we're in haste. We need to find the necklace in ten days. Her voice had an urge, and her eyes looked painful. 'If you know anything or anyone, please let us know.'

Aryan noticed helplessness in her voice. Her urge seemed more out of desperation than candour. It was unlike her. Firdaus was amongst the observers; she would study a person's character before asking for favours, thought Aryan. He stared into her eyes and recalled something she had told him in the past. 'If you want to know the truth, look into their eyes. If they're nervous, they're lying.'

'While researching, I had the privilege to talk to the prince's nephew. I wanted some information on the Patiala Necklace. As far as my memory goes, his family was reluctant to talk about the necklace, let alone its disappearance or current whereabouts. It seemed as if the necklace had only brought a curse to their family. Although it was a family heirloom, particularly expensive and one of a kind, the necklace only brought prying eyes and jealous hearts into the family. They were happy it was gone. Nobody knows where the necklace is. Some say the British stole it, and some believe the royal family hid the marvel from the rest of the world. It could be anywhere from a secret vault beneath their palace to the deepest ocean. Who knows?'

'Do you know the prince's nephew personally? Can you arrange a meeting for us?' Aryan lightly nudged Firdaus, gesturing not to push too hard.

'I don't know him personally. Sorry.'

'Can you try to remember how you met with the prince's family? Who introduced you to them? Are you still in contact with any of them?'

'I wish I could help you, Firdaus, but as you know, my memory is weak. I don't remember much these days. By the way, did I ask you for some tea? Oh god, I forgot, didn't I?'

'It's okay, Ms DeMello, we don't need anything.' Aryan assured. 'No, my dear, let me bring you tea or would you prefer coffee?'

Aryan waited for Firdaus to reply, but she kept her posture intact and mouth shut, so he replied, 'Tea sounds good, Ms DeMello, thanks a lot.'

As soon as Ms DeMello plodded to the kitchen, Aryan turned to Firdaus and berated her for being too direct and unsympathetic. 'She is old and fragile; what were you thinking, Firdaus? Don't you have any compassion?'

'What do you want me to do, listen to her stories? We have no lead so far and less time than before.' Her voice came through her clenched teeth.

'It was your idea to come here, wasn't it?' He snapped. 'Yes, it was, and if you let me do what I am doing, this trip would not be a complete waste of time.'

'Why is it so important for you to find this necklace? I know you don't care about the pride and whatever bullshit you sold to Ram in the office.' He came chillingly close to her face and held her hand tightly.

'Tell me, why do you want to find this necklace?'

She took her hand away from his. 'Stop it!' Her voice was muffled. 'Aryan, please don't ask me stupid questions.' She sighed and turned her anguished face to his.

'Firdaus, you have to tell me the truth.'

'You won't let it go, will you?' She grunted.

Pearl returned, holding a tray in one hand and her book in another. She gave the book to Firdaus. 'Read this when you have the time.' She placed the tray on the table and settled back on her chair. 'You're in luck. I remember the person who introduced me to the prince's nephew.'

Firdaus slid to the edge of the sofa. 'Oh really?' She was surprised. 'Yes, her name is Mrinalini Desai.'

'Where can we find her?'

'She is in Ahmedabad. But let me warn you, she is a tough lady to crack.'

'That's fine. I'll get her to talk.' Firdaus bounced from her seat and hugged her. 'Thank you very much, Pearl.'

'I am happy I could help you. Mariam was like a daughter to me, which means you're like my grandchild.'

'My mother was very fond of you. Now I know why.'

Aryan couldn't understand if she was being genuine or just flattering her for her cause. 'Alright, we must take your leave. Thanks for having us, ' Aryan said, getting up from the sofa. Pearl gave a brief nod to Aryan and then turned to Firdaus. 'I'll pray for your mother's soul,' Pearl said.

'That is very kind of you.' Firdaus hugged her one more time before heading to the door.

'Have a safe trip, and best of luck with your hunt for the lost Necklace.' DeMello waved them goodbye.

* * *

Firdaus got off the cab and stood under the old bridge. It was dawn by the time she had convinced herself to come up with a plan B in case asking people for information didn't work out. She wore a black jacket above dark blue denim and braided her hair so neatly that her forehead seemed bigger than usual. The setting sun flashed the yellowish-orange light on her face, making her honey-toned eyes glisten. Aryan couldn't take his eyes off her. He was mesmerised by her beauty. Her charm was so strong for him to resist.

'She'll be yours if you try again,' his heart whispered. 'Don't forget she betrayed you,' his mind took over. 'If she did it once, she'll do it again.' He thought. He quickly shook his head to snap out of his thoughts and shifted his focus on finding out what Firdaus was up to.

Aryan hid behind the bus station across from where Firdaus was standing. His spot allowed a clear view of the opposite side. He saw Firdaus getting into a black Range Rover, and desperate to know where she was headed, he followed her.

'Hello, Firdaus, it's been a long time. Said an unattractive man sitting next to her in the car.'

'Yes. I know.' She replied bluntly.

'So, you found your way back to the business? How fascinating.'

'I would like to travel in silence. If you don't mind.'

'Don't do this. We have been friends for years now.'

She gave him an acerbic look. 'Calling us friends is an over statement, maybe colleagues or opponents sound more suitable for our relationship.'

'Oh, Firdaus, you haven't changed at all. You're a tigress, as always, ready to bring out your claws and pounce at every opportunity you get.'

'Can we skip the chit-chat? I am really not interested in talking to you. It's high time that you learn to read the room.'

The man sighed. 'Alright. I was just excited to see you. That's all.' The man moved his hand closer to hers and wrapped his fingers against her palm. She whipped out her hand. 'Stop it. You repulse me.' She muttered.

'I don't want to misbehave. I just missed you.' He passed a cocky smile.

'Just shut up, or I swear I'll punch you.' Her eyes bulged in rage.

'Well, go ahead. I don't think you have it in you anymore.'

'Try me and see what I got.' She shot back.

'Okay, calm down. Jesus! You're on fire'. The guy gave up and moved his hand away from hers. Firdaus looked out and gazed at the purple sky. She couldn't stop thinking about Aryan. He had once turned her world upside down, and she had a feeling that was going to happen again.

The SUV stopped outside an abandoned bar in the corner of the town. The bar hardly had any lights, just one above the board that said, 'Eagle's Point.' Firdaus and the man who accompanied her walked through the small gate next to the bar.

Aryan got off the rickshaw a few meters away from the bar and saw Firdaus entering the bar from that small gate. He tried to chase her, but the door shut in seconds. He tried to unlock the door but failed. He glanced around and strode to the back of the building, where he found a water pipe that led him to the roof. He swiftly climbed up and peeked through a hole on the terrace that gave him a partial view of the interior.

Firdaus was sitting on a stool opposite the bar.

'Hi Firdaus, would you like to get the usual?' The bartender asked. 'No, Bob, I am good. Thanks.'

He turned around and poured whisky into two glasses. He offered one to the guy who came with Firdaus and kept the other on the table. A well-built, broad-shouldered man in a black suit entered the bar and sat next to Firdaus.

'What brings you here, Firdaus?' He asked in his hoarse voice.

'I am looking for something, Black Jack.' She opened her handbag and took out a photograph of the Patiala necklace. Once a black-market dealer, Black Jack had now become the Goan crime lord. He featured an intensely diabolical face and a wrestler's body tough enough to knock out anyone.

'I am looking for this necklace. Do you know where I can find it?' She pointed at the jewellery in the photo.

Black Jack took the photo from her hand and stared at it with a poker face. 'You know I don't work for free.'

'Yes, I have got the money. Tell me how much you want?'

'Ten Lakh Rupees.' Black Jack replied.

Firdaus opened her bag and took out an envelope. She handed it to him.

'So, how are you doing, Firdaus?' He asked, counting the cash.

'I am alright.' She replied. 'So, will you do it?' She asked skeptically.

'I'll, but you'll have to do something for me in return.'

Firdaus understood what he wanted even before he asked. 'I don't do that anymore.' She replied solemnly. 'I lost a lot of money when you decided to quit, now that you're back, you'll have to make it up to me.' 'I am not back. I am here only because I need a favour.' She clarified. 'Just do it this one time, for me.' Black Jack slid the envelope towards her. 'I don't want your money. I want you to fight. If you want my help, this is what it'll take.' He got up and walked to her. 'So, will you fight? Firdaus sighed. 'Do I have a choice?' 'You better win if you want to find the necklace.' He whispered in her ears.

The bar quickly filled up with a cheering crowd as Black Jack announced a boxing match between Mojo, short for Manjusri, a regular boxer and Firdaus. The crowd waved cash and yelled out the name of the boxer they wanted to bet on. Black Jack settled on his seat in front of the crowd and gestured to the referee to begin the match. Mojo and Firdaus tested each other by glaring at one another. Mojo looked fierce and determined to win. Her athletic body moved with finesse as she stretched before entering the ring. On the other hand, Firdaus's body language was hard to decode. She looked nervous and pale. Her body was equally athletic but appeared a little stiff due to lack of practice. 'Okay, let's do this.' She told herself.

Mojo blew a punch in the air as Firdaus astutely pulled her head back, but before she could punch back, Mojo landed a good blow on her stomach. Firdaus stooped and stepped back. She squealed in pain when Mojo hit her spine, dropping her to the floor. The stink of stale beer filled her nostrils. She snorted and wiped the blood flowing out of her nose as she got up. Mojo was facing the cheering crowd, showing off her victory, and taking that opportunity, Firdaus struck from behind, blowing a punch at her jaw. Mojo stumbled and fell flat on the floor. Firdaus pushed her knee hard into her stomach until Mojo gave up. Mojo won the first round and second was claimed by Firdaus, the whistle blew, and the last round began. The cheering crowd went silent and people who bet on Mojo started biting their nails.

Equipped with the latest techniques and professional training, Mojo had the upper hand over Firdaus, who had hardly boxed in three years. Leveraging her skills, she hit Firdaus below the belt, where she knew it would hurt her the most. Firdaus groaned in pain but didn't give up. She took a few deep breaths and a moment to decide her next move. She used the check hook technique to counterpunch Mojo. Mojo held her from the waist and dragged her back until Firdaus regained her balance and pulled out. Firdaus knew she was out of time and needed to do something to win the match, so she progressed aggressively towards Mojo and when Mojo tried to catch her, she ducked and caught her by her waist. She dragged her to the edge of the ring when Mojo loosened her arm to catch the ring, Firdaus grabbed her by the neck and threw her on the ground. Mojo tried to get back on her feet as the referee began the countdown, but Firdaus held her tight until she was declared the winner.

The crowd sighed at once, and the bar fell silent. Firdaus turned her head to Black Jack, who got up from his seat to applaud. 'I won twenty lakhs today because of you.' He offered her a glass of scotch. 'Take, it'll help with the pain.' Firdaus took out the ice cubes from the glass and wrapped them into a towel to apply on her bruised eyes. As the ice touched her reddened face, she felt a moment of relief from the burning pain that numbed her cheeks. She gulped the drink to calm her jittery nerves and settled back on the bar chair to conduct her business.

'This is important, Black Jack, and time-sensitive, too. You'll have to find the necklace in the next forty-eight hours.'

'Are you in trouble, Firdaus?' He asked. 'My troubles are none of your business. I didn't get my ass kicked just now, so we can chit-chat. Just do what I asked you to do.'

'Understood! You'll get your information in forty-eight hours.'

Watching her leave the bar, Aryan got off the roof and followed her to the main road. He was now convinced there was more to the story than what Firdaus told initially, and he was determined to find out.

Firdaus…. Firdaus wait, he yelled.

'What are you doing here, Aryan?'

'I should be asking you that question, Firdaus.' Firdaus's face sulked. 'I don't have to answer you.' She turned around so that she didn't have to face him.

'Look at me, will you!' Aryan pulled her close to him. 'Let go of me.' She jerked to step back.

'Why are you after the necklace? Tell me the truth.' He urged.

'It was my mother's dream.' She said with teary eyes. 'That necklace was important to her. She wanted to find it. I am just', she stuttered, 'trying to fulfil her last wish. That's all.' She snorted and wiped her nose.

Aryan saw through her and instantly knew she was lying. He had known her enough to read her mind.

'Firdaus, how can you be so ruthless? How can you lie to my face so shamelessly?

'I am sorry, Aryan; I can't tell you the truth. It'll only ruin your life as it has ruined mine.

They wished they could say this to each other, but their silence spoke more than all the words they had exchanged so far. Aryan's face turned grim, and eyes widened in anger. 'I know you're lying.' He came chillingly close to her, making her heartbeat pulsate through her chest. 'I won't let you wrong me this time.' His words suffocated her; she couldn't breathe or gulp and felt like running far away from his warm breath that strangled her. She turned around and looked into his eyes. She felt his face close to hers and her lips an inch away from his. She shut her eyes, letting her tears dampen her cheeks and then her lips as Aryan kissed her. Both let go of their emotions in that fleeting moment of passion, only to realise it was a mistake a minute later.

Aryan shrugged and stepped back. 'What am I doing?' He murmured. Firdaus narrowed her eyes and looked down. 'We should go now.' She said softly.

* * *

Firdaus threw her bag on the bed and dropped herself to the floor. She shut her eyes and took a few deep breaths. Her emotions had crippled her; she silently cursed the moment she had agreed to work with Aryan knowing his presence would only complicate things. She exhaled loudly to snap out of her misery, but nothing aided her pain. Her suffering, both physical and emotional, stifled her and she couldn't hold back from picking up the phone.

'Hello, Firdaus!' A hollow voice came through the phone.

'Where are you?'

'Why is that important to you?'

'It is, you know that.'

Debojeet gave no answer.

'Listen, I'll find the Patiala Necklace soon.'

'Good to hear.' He replied.

'I am going to Ahmedabad to meet someone.'

'I don't care, Firdaus, who you meet or who you kill. I want THE Necklace, that's all.'

'I know the deal, Debojeet.'

'Then why have you called? Want something?'

'Ye-es,' Her tongue became heavy. 'Can I talk to her?' Debojeet didn't respond. 'Please let me talk to her.' Firdaus insisted but didn't get any response from him. She waited for a minute. 'Hi, Mumma. How are you?' An innocent voice emerged from the phone. 'Hi, my darling, I missed you so much,' Firdaus's eyes filled with tears. 'Mumma loves you; you know that, right.' She said. 'Yes, Mumma, I miss you too.' Her heart sank as those words got out of her daughter's mouth. Ariana, her daughter, was too far. She was abducted, and the only way to get her back was to find the Patiala Necklace.

Chapter 4

Ahmedabad

Aryan wasn't happy with the deal Firdaus had made with Black Jack. He was convinced it would only lead them to more problems. To him, Black Jack didn't seem like a man who could be trusted. When Firdaus told him that Black Jack would find the Necklace for them, he refused to believe her and instead he suggested going to Ahmedabad to meet Mrs Mrinalini Desai.

Firdaus had no choice but to yield to his adjuring. There was no way she could have convinced Aryan to work with Black Jack, and she knew that if she persisted, she would have to tell him the truth. So, she agreed to Aryan's plan to pursue Ms DeMello's lead, and so they went to Ahmedabad.

Mrs Mrinalini Desai's residence was surrounded by closely packed houses, led by narrow, meandering streets that opened in a big Chowk—an area popularly called 'Dhal ni Pol' in the local language. Aryan was silent throughout their journey since he had no desire for further failure in his truth-seeking endeavour. Firdaus, on the other hand, indulged in many conversations, totally unrelated to the hunt, to divert her mind from her daughter's abduction.

'Did you know the pol city of Ahmedabad is listed as one of the world heritage sites by UNESCO?' Firdaus spoke with curiosity.

'Oh, so are we talking again and not fighting? That's new.' He said, taking a jibe at her.

'Aryan, will you ever stop with those taunts?' Aryan kept quiet, trying not to aggravate the situation.

'No,' she murmured. 'Thought so.'

'If you tell me the truth, then maybe I'll be able to help you more efficiently.'

Oh, no need. You're doing more than enough.'

'Firdaus, wait. Stop here.' Aryan held her hand. 'Why can't you tell me the truth? You don't trust me?'

'Aryan, you know that this is not about me trusting you, if at all it's the other way around.' She sighed.

'So, you're admitting that there is more to the story than you're letting on.'

'I have admitted to no such thing. Please, Aryan, stop wasting your time.' Firdaus started walking on.

'If I were you, I would focus on finding an idea to convince Mrs Desai to help us.' She smirked.

Finally, after ten minutes of walking uphill, they made it to Mrinalini Desai's residence. The intricately carved, red-painted wooden door was charming. Firdaus leaned over to see the interior that looked colourful. The wall supporting the veranda was painted green and etched with designs and patterns inspired by Rajputana Mahals. Aryan pressed the arch-shaped door knocker and waited for the resident to open the door.

A short- heightened man opened the door and began communicating in Gujarati. 'Who are you?' He asked in his native language.

'Sorry, neither of us speaks Gujarati.' Firdaus replied.

'What do you want?' The man asked in Hindi. 'We're here to meet Mrs Mrinalini Desai.' Aryan replied.

'Oh, do you have an appointment?' He asked politely. 'No, we don't.' 'Yes, we do.' Firdaus intervened. We're from Frequent Traveller's magazine. We're doing an article on the heritage city of Ahmedabad, and we have been told that Mrs Desai is very influential and is also willing to share information on the local culture.

Aryan gave her a loathsome look for lying but soon realized it was the only way to get in, so he played along. The short man smiled and welcomed them in. 'You're from the press. Many people from newspapers and radios often come to visit Mrs Desai.' He gloated.

'That's interesting!' Firdaus replied.

Observing the traditional and vernacular architecture of the low-rise adorned with various religious artifacts, she thought of the occupant as opulent, elegant and a person of faith. They were escorted to the living room and asked to take a seat. 'Let me talk to her. I am sure she'll appreciate honesty.' Aryan whispered to Firdaus. 'Go ahead, be my guest.'

The lady of the house walked into the room in a loose cotton kaftan. The 50- year-old had a curvy body held by broad shoulders. Her pale skin tone failed to compliment her dark black hair that she had probably dyed. Desai's appearance wasn't particularly charming, but her persona oozed magnificence as if she had harboured long years of challenges that usually come with an elaborate political career. Firdaus had noticed her posters and billboards across the city on her way up to her abode. Her canvassing was prominent enough to catch the eyes of everyone passing through. She was polling for the post of chief minister in the upcoming state elections.

'Hello, Ma'am. My name is Aryan Verma, and she is my colleague, Firdaus.' Mrinalini looked at Firdaus and smiled.

'Firdaus is a beautiful name. Are you a Muslim?'

'Yes, half though, my dad was a Muslim and my mom Catholic.'

'Oh, I see.' A long and intense pause followed, making Firdaus even more uncomfortable. 'Are you a woman of faith, Ms Firdaus?' She asked, breaking the silence.

'I am afraid not. But I wouldn't deny or argue with the beliefs of others.'

'Aha, so you're an atheist!' Mrinalini looked at her with curiosity. She gazed into her eyes deep enough to reach her soul. Firdaus coughed to distract her. 'I would prefer to talk about something else if you don't mind.' She suggested out of discomfort. Mrinalini kept her gaze intact. 'Madam, we are looking for the Patiala Necklace.' Aryan interrupted. 'I am an ASI officer, and Ms Durrani is an art dealer; we were told you could help us.

'Help you how?' Desai asked, moving her eyes from Firdaus to Aryan.

Firdaus immediately regretted her decision to stay silent. She could sense that they were going to be thrown out of the house in seconds. 'We would like to meet the nephew of the late Prince of Patiala.' Firdaus dropped her face into her hands.

'I was told you both are journalists.'

'No, ma'am, we are not.' Aryan replied sheepishly.

She exhaled a breath that filled the room with tension. 'I admire your candour, Mr Verma, but sadly, whoever told you that I was of any help was mistaken. I was once close to Prince's nephew, but that was long ago.' She took a pause and glanced through the room before continuing. 'I am not obligated to help you but take my advice if you want. The Patiala necklace disappeared years ago. I am sure it's gone, perhaps dismantled, and fed to hawks and vultures of the world.' Firdaus and Aryan failed to prolong the conversation. They heard what she said, and there was nothing more for them to ask. Firdaus thought Aryan would be more persistent with his request for answers, but his silence faltered their plan. 'I think we are done here. Moti will escort you out.' Said Mrinalini, getting up from her sofa.

'Why do I have to deal with this imbecile?' Firdaus yelled in her brain.

'I am sorry.' Aryan whispered. Firdaus nodded and kept walking. 'So, what now?' Aryan asked nervously.

'I don't know, but I'll figure it out,' she crisply replied. Firdaus brisked her pace on the downhill road. Aryan thought she was trying to get away from him, so he followed her at an equal pace. 'Firdaus, I said, I am sorry.'

She turned around and blurted, 'stop apologizing, Aryan. I would love to gloat over my idea and tell you I told you so', but unfortunately, this is not the time for it. We need information from her, and I need to think how.'

'Do you need my help?'

'No, you have done enough. I'll try to meet her alone. She seemed intrigued by me. Couldn't tell if she liked something about me or took offence at my atheism. But either way, she'll talk to me. I have an instinct about her.'

Aryan passed a faint smile, 'well then, I'll see you at the hotel.'

As soon as she saw Aryan hailing a cab, she took out her phone from her handbag and called Debojeet. 'I need urgent intel on someone.' She said authoritatively. 'I am not your errand boy.' He sharply replied.

'I would have used my sources, but the chance of getting help from them is meagre; they are not as resourceful as you are.'

'All I hear is excuses.' 'How about you call me next when you have the Necklace and from the burner phone, I gave you.' Firdaus frustratingly punched her fist on her forehead. 'Debojeet, you're leaving me with no choice but to seek help from Aryan, and he'll make the first call to the CBI.'

'I told you, no CBI.'

'Then help me. Give me some dirt on Mrs Mrinalini Desai. She is running for state elections. I am sure she'll have skeletons in her closet that I can threaten to expose.' She sounded persistent.

'Fine, I'll call you back in fifteen minutes.' Debojeet hung up.

Aryan punched his room key card multiple times on the digital lock outside the room, but the door did not open. 'Can you open my room? It seems I kept the key card too close to my cell phone.' A chuckle followed his request. The gap-toothed housekeeping guy opened the door with the master key card he possessed. 'A lot of people do that, sir.' The housekeeping boy announced. 'Thank you so much, Gaurav.' Aryan said, reading the name card buckled on his shirt.

'You're welcome, sir.' He replied with a smile and dragged his cleaning cart to the next room.

Aryan shut the door and began snooping through Firdaus's belongings. He pulled the drawer, hoping to find her passport or wallet, but all he found were tourism pamphlets provided by the hotel. Her luggage bag was lightweight and filled with clothes, toiletries, and shoes. Finally, he swung open the closet and found a locker under the left-hand shelf. He tried unlocking it several times with codes he could think of, but after three failed attempts, he took his phone and texted his ex-colleague, Mihir Agnihotri.

'Hi! Need a favour.' He typed and sent. 'What is the universal unlocking code for Tempton lockers?' He asked in a text. In a few seconds, his friend replied. 'It's 0011.'

'Thanks a lot.' Aryan texted back and got a reply saying, 'We should talk sometime.'

'Yes, not just that, we should meet too. I have heard you got a promotion.' Aryan typed, but before sending the message, he deleted it and sent a smile emoji instead.

He selected the numbers on the locker, and a click sound followed. The Locker had Firdaus's passport, a burner phone, bundles of cash and a gun. Lots of cash stacked in piles and the presence of a pistol petrified Aryan. He flipped through the cash bundle, trembling with fear. These were things only a criminal would carry, he thought. 'God Firdaus, what have you got us into.' He sighed. He shut the locker and sat on the floor. Drops of sweat drizzled from his temples. He wiped them off with his hand and took out his phone from his pocket. 'Can I ask for another favour?' He typed.

'Yes, please go ahead.' Mihir replied.

'I am sending you a picture of a rifle that looks like a licensed handgun. Can you tell me under whose name it is registered?'

'It seems ASI is giving you some rough tasks.' Mihir joked.

'No, this is personal. I need the information as soon as possible.'

'I'll look up now. Give me five minutes.' He answered.

Firdaus plodded through the Chowk, observing the enthralling architecture of the Pol city. She was just passing her time waiting for Debojeet to get back with something she could use to extort information from Mrs Desai. She checked her phone every few minutes, waiting for him to call. Finally, after half an hour, he called and said, 'I couldn't find a lot on your woman, but there is this one thing that might work. Most of her campaign money comes from Mahalaxmi Builders, who have recently acquired land that belonged to some farmers. And she helped him acquire the land?' Firdaus interrupted. 'Yes, illegally. These farmers have filed a court case against the builder. Perfect, I believe this will work.' Exhaling a sigh of relief, she thanked him and hung up the phone.

The short-sighted man returned to the door. "Did you leave something behind, Ms?' He asked.

'No, I just need to talk to Mrs Desai. It's urgent.'

'I am sorry. I can't let you come in now.'

'Please, Moti Ji,' she respectfully pleaded. 'It is crucial. Can you ask her if she is willing to see me for just a few minutes? I won't take much of her time. I promise.'

'Okay, wait here. I'll ask her if she wants to meet you.' Said he, rushing to her room. After a few minutes, he returned with a smile on his face. 'Please come in. She'll see you now.'

This time, she was escorted to Mrs Desai's balcony. The beautiful space was adorned with flowering plants and antique furniture. It overlooked a narrow street that traversed through a couple of shops and a small temple that fostered reverence in the passing crowd, making them bow their heads in respect. In the distance stood a mosque that called out the afternoon Azan (call for prayer). She heard it when she entered the balcony. 'Let us wait for the prayers to finish.' Desai insisted. She pointed at the chair opposite her and asked Firdaus to take a seat.

Aryan relentlessly paced through the room, waiting for his friend to text back. His heart pounded every time his phone beeped. Finding a gun in her closet had freaked him out, and thoughts of her being involved in some nefarious affairs had haunted him ever since. 'I wouldn't let her get away with her schemes this time.' He told himself. Upon hearing his phone beep again, he flounced to pick up the device he had thrown on the bed out of anger. The text read, 'the gun belongs to Mr Debojeet Bagchi'.

'Who the hell is Debojeet Bagchi, and why is Firdaus carrying his gun?' He thought. I must confront Firdaus and compel her to tell me the truth. He announced loudly to himself.

'You know why I am here, Mrs Desai.' She said confidently.

'You are wasting your time, young lady. I have told you I don't know where the Necklace is.'

'Well, I am sure you have doubts about its whereabouts, but you know the family who owned it. All I want from you is to call Prince Amrendra Singh's nephew Ajit Singh and organize a rendezvous.'

Sneering at her request, she said, 'Why would I do that?'

'Because you want to save your political career. Don't you? I know about the court case and the land acquisition; I'll expose it to the media, and they'll have a field trip.'

Mrinalini's face turned grim, 'I don't respond to threats, Ms Durrani. Don't you think many like yourself would have tried, but Mrinalini Desai is not so vulnerable! Go, do whatever you want with your information; I don't care.' She replied, grimacing at her appalling tactics.

Firdaus kept her gaze still and posture confident. 'I am sorry, Mrs Desai, how about we start fresh? I already regret blackmailing you. I have no interest in ruining your political career, and I am now assured that badgering you would not help either. So, how about quid pro quo! You help me, and I help you in return.'

'I don't need any help, Ms Firdaus, especially not from an amateur like yourself.' Seconds of silence followed her remark. Mrinalini got up from her seat and strolled through the balcony. 'Firdaus, you seem like an ambitious young woman with the right intellect. You intrigued me this morning, but sadly, your lack of passion and superficial blackmailing tactics proved me wrong. You're not who I assumed you were.'

'She is right. I am off my game,' Firdaus brooded. I should have known better than coming here underprepared.' Her lack of preparation had shrunk her chances of extracting any information from her. She knew she was in the lion's den, and she had to make her way out unscathed. 'I know why you refuse to help me, ' she declared, keeping her gaze still and posture undefeated.

'How can you betray a confidante you claim to love?' Mrinalini paused her pace and turned to Firdaus, her scowling face crying, 'how dare you?'

Firdaus felt victorious in that instance, exposing her opponent's vulnerability by fluke. 'So, it's true, ' she gloated. Now, you'll tell me where the necklace is, or I'll expose your illicit love affair with Ajit Singh to the media.'

'I don't know where it is.' She replied nervously.

'Then get me acquainted with the one who knows. 'Her relentless intimidation was unnerving the politician. Mrinalini's perception of her as a harmless amateur had backfired. Her career, marriage and political aspirations were all in jeopardy now that someone else had the information about her affair. 'You won't be able to prove anything.' 'Oh, I don't have to. What are reporters for? She smiled.

'Alright! I'll make a call to Ajit.' She agreed. 'You can go meet him in Udaipur the day after tomorrow.'

'Thank you, Mrs Desai. I appreciate your help.'

'He won't give you the necklace even if he has it, and blackmailing wouldn't work on him.'

'You assumed that about yourself, too, but sadly, you yielded. Ajit would too.' Firdaus said confidently. A sense of victory had taken away her pain, and she finally felt like herself again. Ferocious Firdaus is back! She roared. Her face looked more radiant and refreshed, as if a fresh blood flow had traversed her nerves. She galloped like a little child walking down the lane.

On the other hand, Mrinalini's face flushed with her boiling blood. She clenched her fist and shoved it in her mouth to control her anger. The revelation of her affair not only threatened her chances of winning the election but would also end her almost non-existent marriage that brought her to politics. This horrid thought of a doomed career and lonely existence made her anxious. 'Moti, go and get my anti-anxiety pills.' She yelled in exasperation. The short-heighted errand boy rushed to her room to grab the pills. Taking a few shuddering breaths, she grabbed her phone and dialled a number.

'Hello! We have a problem!' She said sombrely.

Firdaus placed her bag into the security machine. She walked towards the tall security guard whose job was to hover his portable metal scanner around people before letting them pass.

'Namaste, madam! Please welcome.' The guard said, joining his hands.

'Thank you very much.' She replied.

Aryan furiously paced through the hotel lobby, waiting for Firdaus to return. When he saw her coming in, he fumingly rushed to her and stopped her. He held her arm tightly. 'Firdaus, come with me.' He said from his clenched teeth.

'Why are you woofing, Aryan? Take it easy. I have got good news for both of us.' She replied, trying to calm him down. He did not listen to her and dragged her with him towards the elevator. 'What is your problem, Aryan? Leave my hand. You're hurting me.' She cried.

'Just shut up, Firdaus. For once, keep quiet and come with me.'

Aryan did not let go of her arm and held it tightly. 'I am not going anywhere. I'll come with you. Just let go of my arm.' She winced. He dragged her to his room and threw her onto the bed. 'What the hell Aryan? What are you doing?' She asked nervously, confused by Aryan's temperamental behaviours.

'Now, you'll tell me the truth and nothing else. I won't let you leave this room until you tell me what is going on with you.'

'I have told you the truth, Aryan, and if you choose not to believe it, that's your problem.' She said gruffly.

'I found a burner phone and a gun in your locker. That gun belongs to someone called Debojeet Bagchi. Can you explain who he is and how is he involved in this hunt of yours?' Firdaus flinched hearing the name. 'No, I mean, yes, he is actually a friend.' She fumbled. 'Stop lying, Firdaus. Just stop it.' His fingers pressed her cheeks so hard that her nose and cheekbones turned red.

'Aryan, please let go of me. You're hurting me.' She pleaded with tears in her eyes. He quickly took his hand off her face and moved back.

'You bring out the worst in me,' Firdaus. 'You turn me into an animal. I don't like myself when I am with you. Your existence disgusts me.' He cried, regretting his behaviour.

'Aryan, I am sorry, but believe me, what I have told you is the truth.' Her voice became faint.

'I don't believe you, and you know that quite well. What you did five years ago broke me, and how you're lying to my face right now is hurting even more.

'I understand, and I have apologized many times for what I did five years ago. You tell me, how many more sorries will it take for us to make amends?'

'Nothing you do or say will change how I think of you,' he yelled, punching the wall with his knuckles.

She got up from the bed and motioned towards the corner where Aryan was standing. Holding his hand, she said, 'Aryan, I promise I'll tell you everything when the time is right. For now, finding the Necklace is my priority because my life depends on it.'

Unclasping his fingers, he swiftly moved his hand away from hers and said, 'I have no choice but to do as you say because I need my job. He raised his finger at her. Remember, this is not over yet, and you must not think you can get away with this. I'll find the truth in time.'

'I am sure you'll, now, please come to Rajasthan with me. We have a meeting with the prince's nephew the day after tomorrow.

Mrinalini Desai asked her security guards to stay at the gate and entered the restaurant alone. The restaurant was empty and scarcely staffed. It was their closing time, but the owner had asked some employees to stay back and attend to the future Chief Minister of Gujarat. She was welcomed and escorted to the terrace, where a table filled with the finest local cuisine awaited her.

A petite lady in her early fifties was relishing the fermented and steamed sour cake entrée called Dhoklas in Gujarati. 'Gujarati food is so delicious.' She said, licking her fingers.

'I am glad you ate well because what I am going to say will shrink your appetite. Mrinalini dropped her purse on the table and settled across from the lady.

'Yes, go ahead. I am listening.' The petite lady replied.

'It is about Firdaus Durrani. She and the ASI are looking for the Patiala Necklace.' She summarized. Maria Saldana called the waiter and asked him to bring her a finger bowl. 'You don't look surprised. It seems you already know about this.'

'I had a hunch, and my men confirmed it. However, I had no idea Firdaus was involved.' A short pause followed, and the room turned silent.

'She is resolute and won't back down.' Mrinalini said, breaking the silence. 'I know, you don't worry, I'll handle this.' Maria Saldana replied solemnly.

'Elections are around the corner, and I don't want any troubles from Firdaus or the ASI. The Patiala Necklace should remain hidden at all costs, and I need you to do everything you can to stop that girl from finding it. And if you fail in doing so, I'll have to handle her myself, and you won't like that.'

'I know my job well, Mrinalini. So, calm down and let me take care of it.'

Mrinalini exhaled a sigh. 'It has been a very long day. I must take your leave now. But you can finish your dinner. I have heard the food here is good.' Maria nodded in approval. 'Sure, it is.'

Mrinalini snapped her fingers at the waiter, gesturing for him to come to their table. 'Get a glass of Chaas (spicy buttermilk) for our guest.' She ordered and then got up to leave. 'Mrinalini, all the best for the elections.' Maria raised her thumb. After bidding farewell to the politician, she called Mihir Agnihotri, a junior R&AW agent. She ordered him to track Firdaus and her partner and find out what they were up to.

Chapter 5

Tashkent, Uzbekistan

Karim Khan rested his head on the back of his car seat and shut his eyes for a bit. His temples burnt with a throbbing pain caused by Migraine. Karim had two hours to rest before the big meeting for which he had travelled to Uzbekistan from Abu Dhabi. He took out a small box from the pocket of his jacket and popped two pills from it before going off to sleep. Within five minutes of shutting his eyes, he fell fast asleep, and ten minutes into sleeping, his worst nightmare returned.

There was fire everywhere: the roof was on fire, the doors were burning, and the flames fumed out of the window like they were coming straight out of a dragon's mouth. A little boy stood behind the tree outside the house and watched the uniformed men light the house on fire. It wasn't just the house they meant to burn; it was the little boy's whole family. His father was shot dead, and his mother was left to burn alive. The screeching sound of her yelling blustered through the deep woods of Baramulla, but no one came to help. Every bit of his body wanted to save his mother, but the boy couldn't move. He was scared of being caught and killed. Drops of sweat circled his forehead as he peed in his pants. Karim wanted to shout to let go of his pain; he wanted to cry for not being able to save his family, but all he did was hide. The sight of the full-blown inferno never left his mind, and the burning fire that killed his family settled deep into his heart.

The meeting was convened in a huge corridor of an unoccupied 17th century palace. Six majestic armchairs were placed around the timber-topped rectangular dining table. Five chairs were identical except for one, which was kept on one end of the table that was reserved for the host. The table was adorned with three candle stands decorated with gilded bronze arms to hold the candle. The wine decanter was filled with the best fruit wine and the platter on the centre of the table held different meats aromatic enough for everyone to want to devour.

All the five men settled on their designated seats. Two of them possessed dark hair and beards and wore sedate suits. They spoke in Arabic with each other. The third man was a local and wore the uniform of a local law enforcement officer. The fourth man was a blonde with grey eyes, an American. His blue suit was too well tailored, and mannerisms too proper for anyone to guess he was from the CIA. The fifth was a grey-haired European. All the middle-aged men poured their drinks and waited for the host to arrive.

Karim Khan woke up with a headache worse than what he had slept with. The nightmare had dragged the 60-year-old back into the mind of the 15-year-old who stood helpless outside of the burning house. The pain he endured as a child only grew with age, and his suffering became a source of his vendetta. Khan whisked to the bathroom to splash some cold water on his face. He pulled out his small metal box and gulped another two pills, this time without a glass of water.

A black limousine stopped outside the Palace, and Karim got out of it in his finest black suit. As he walked towards the table, all the five men first turned their heads to welcome him, and then, as he came closer, they all got up to greet him. 'I apologize for being late. I am most delighted to have you all here tonight to discuss the important matter, but before we do that, let us indulge in this luxurious dining experience and let our palates taste these delectable local delicacies.' Everyone raised a toast to Karim's announcement and began to eat.

* * *

Abu Dhabi

Ariana sulked and refused to go to sleep without hearing her favorite story. Her caretaker came up with many different ideas to get her to sleep. She gave her warm milk, a head massage and half an hour of screen time, but the child clung to her doll and refused to sleep. Finally, her babysitter gave up and went to Debojeet for help.

When Bagchi came into the room, Ariana jumped from her bed and shouted, 'where is my mom? I want her now.'

'Ariana' Bagchi called her with a loving voice. 'Your mom will come soon and when she comes, she will want to see you happy and in good health.'

Ariana sat on the bed again. 'When will she come?' There was an urge in the child's voice.

'She'll come soon, my child.' Bagchi replied, settling next to her on the bed. 'Now, I hear you want to listen to your favourite story?' Ariana nodded. 'Yes, the little princess and her sheep.' 'Well, how about we hear a different story tonight?' The girl contemplated for a minute but then agreed. 'Is it a princess story?' She asked curiously. 'No, it is a story of two monkeys.'

'I don't want to hear the story of two monkeys.' She made a face.

'I promise, you'll like it more than your princess stories.'

'Really?'

'Yes, now close your eyes and listen to me.'

'Once upon a time, there were two monkeys; one was called Muro, and the other one was Shubo.' Ariana kept her head next to Bagchi's and laid down to hear the rest of the story. 'Both Muro and Shubo were orphans; they had no family and no one who loved or cared for them, so they became friends and decided to stick together come what may. Muro was fierce, strong and determined, and Shubo was calm and intelligent. Both set out in the open sea to find the treasure. For Muro, finding the treasure was a rebellion, but for Shubo, it was survival. They fought with all the demons who emerged from the depths of the sea to stop them from getting to the treasure. Shubo used to distract them, and Muro would fight ferociously. Ultimately, all the demons died, and both the monkeys reached the treasure alcove. To their dismay, they found the treasure alcove empty besides this one necklace that looked precious.' 'So, who took the necklace, Muro or Shubo?' Ariana asked curiously. 'They both decided to ask the god to choose who gets the treasure. The god decided to test them. The one who succeeds in killing all other animals on the island will be the winner, the god announced. Muro went on a rampage and started killing everyone who came in his way; Shubo, on the other hand, went to the lion and whispered something in his ears. The lion roared in anger and went on a hunt. He lunged on Muro and bit his neck. The Lion roared, 'why're you killing my animals? Muro jumped on the branch of a tree and yelled, 'let me kill them all and I'll spare you.' Lion laughed out of disgust and replied, 'I am the king of this jungle, and you're nothing but a monkey. You can't kill me.' His reply enraged Muro, and he jumped onto the lion, scratching his face. Both the animals fought and killed each other. Shubo passed the test and got the treasure. 'So, what is the moral of the story? Who should we be like, Muro or Shubo?' Ariana widened her eyes out of inquisitiveness. Debojeet smiled. 'This is not a fight between good or bad where it is easy to choose a side; it is between bad and worse. Don't choose a side unless absolutely necessary, and if you must, choose survival.'

'My mom says killing animals is a bad thing. So, both Muro and Shubo did a bad thing.' Ariana said innocently.

'But God put them in a spot like that, where they had no choice.'

'My mom says people always have a choice. I don't think those monkeys should have killed anyone. '

Bagchi held her hand and sighed. 'Sometimes, we don't. And you'll know this when you grow up.'

Her eyes were wide open, and they were gazing at the ceiling. 'You were supposed to sleep after the story.' Said Bagchi. 'I am not sleepy. I want my mom.' 'She'll soon be with you, I promise.'

Bagchi planted a soft kiss on the child's forehead before putting her to sleep.

* * *

Karim Khan took the last sip of wine from his glass and wiped his mouth with the linen cloth kept next to his plate. 'The plan will soon be put into action, but it won't succeed without your help, especially from the CIA.' Khan's voice was strained and wispy. 'The CIA has provided you with enough, now any attack you plan is all on your own. We must not be involved any further.' The American replied, 'I am only asking you to divert the government with other issues so that they fail to see what's coming their way.' 'Our purpose was to provide weapons to you, and we did that; I am afraid we can't help you anymore. The country you're trying to destroy is our ally, and the best I can do for you is to keep my mouth shut and not tell a soul about this meeting.' Khan looked slightly disappointed. 'Well, if that is the best you can offer, I'll take it.'

'Now, can we discuss the matter that concerns us?' One of the Arab guys raised his hand. 'Sure, what is it? 'Khan took a sip of water. 'Uranium!' 'What about it.' 'We need 20 kgs of Uranium, and you know buying and selling it as a commodity is impossible.' 'I'll talk to my source and organise it for you. However, I would need something in return.' The two Arab men looked at each other and then at Karim. 'I want you to test my nuclear weapon in a discreet location. I want to make sure it is in its best form before it meets its destiny.' Whispers spread through the table. 'This is insane.' The European said to the American. 'I know, this has gone out of hand. He is planning a nuclear attack.' The grey-eyed CIA agent whispered in concern. 'We are only here to keep up the chaos; at least, that is my order.' The Austrian felt disgusted and left the room. The Arabs made a call and, a few minutes later, shook hands with Khan. The deal was done, hands were stomped on the table, and Khan was pleased to see one of his agendas succeed in the meeting.

Chapter 6

Mumbai, 5 Years Ago

The renowned jeweller and one of the prominent business tycoons, Nirvaan Kumar had absconded after orchestrating a bank scam and several other income tax thefts. His luxury jewellery store 'Diamond Bazar' was under CBI investigation which was led by Dhimant Thakur and his team. Aryan was a part of his team and was responsible for overseeing the case.

Aryan and his team were asked to confiscate all the diamond jewellery in the store, including bespoke necklaces, earrings, solitaire rings and heaps of shiny stones capable of making all women ecstatic. Aryan pulled a box of rubies out of Nirvaan's locker and kept it next to his colleague, who was accounting for the total amount of jewels recovered. 'Look at these stones. They must be worth millions. What do you think?' Aryan asked.

'I don't know, must be.' His colleague replied with his head buried in the excel sheet he was populating.

'Oh well, I hope it is. That bastard has looted our banks and has now fled like a coward. If his jewellery recovers half of what he has taken, we will be able to save the banks.' Aryan sighed.

As Aryan took one last glance at the store that now resembled a raided site, memories flooded his mind of a time when it had been hailed as the palace of luxury. Contemplating the fleeting nature of good times, he realized that every place eventually earns its charm only to lose it in the end. No matter how arduously one strives, time has an uncanny ability to transform everything it touches.

While glancing through the empty rooms, he saw a gorgeous woman walking towards him. She stopped across from him and asked him if he knew where Dhimant Thakur was. Spellbound by her effortless beauty, Aryan couldn't move or take his eyes off her honey-toned eyes that examined him through glasses.

'Excuse me, do you know where I can find Mr Dhimant Thakur? Firdaus repeated, thinking the guy opposite her would have not heard her the first time. Quickly snapping out of his awe, Aryan responded, 'this way and escorted her to Dhimant.

'Sir, someone is here to meet you.' He said, placing his hands behind his back.

'Firdaus, how are you?' Dhimant offered a handshake.

'I am well, thank you.' She replied.

'Aryan, this is Firdaus Durrani, a freelance auditor, and she is here to provide an accurate valuation for the recovered jewellery.

'Oh, I see. She does look like an auditor, especially with those glasses.' Aryan prattled.

'Firdaus, this is Aryan and Aryan, this is Firdaus'. 'I want you both to work together and sort this mess out as soon as possible.'

'Of course, sir. I'll fill in Ms Durrani and take her through everything.'

'Good!' Dhimant replied and walked away to attend to a phone call.

'So, now that we're working together, can I call you Fifi?' Aryan asked thoughtlessly, only to realize after a second that he had made a complete fool of himself. 'Ah.. My name is Firdaus. Let's just call me that.' She replied bluntly. She then turned around and whispered, 'Fifi' seriously, what was he thinking? Watching her walk away, Aryan turned his head in the opposite direction and called himself foolish, stupid, and half a dozen synonyms. 'Why did I call her Fifi? How dumb am I?' He wondered.

For the next few days, he behaved professionally and only spoke to her if there was a dire need. He showed her the storage facility where the collected treasure was kept and provided a list of retail prices to start auditing. He often attempted to regain his confidence around Firdaus by thinking of asking her out on a date, but after the Fifi fiasco, he had no courage to face her, let alone date. 'Why did I have to say that? He wondered every time he saw her.

Aryan felt nervous and anxious around her. He would often stare at her, and when she would look back, he would take his eyes off her and pretend to do whatever he was doing. Firdaus pitied the guy. He tried too hard to stay out of her way but couldn't do it. So, she decided to jolt him out of his misery. 'Look, Aryan, you don't have to be so nervous around me. I have nothing against you.' Aryan muttered something in a muted voice, probably thanking God for saving him from a perpetual state of embarrassment and turned around to face Firdaus. 'You think I am a fool, don't you?' He asked sheepishly.

'No, I don't. You're a decent person, Aryan, and if you promise never to call me Fifi, then we can be friends,' Firdaus stated sincerely. Aryan chuckled, acknowledging the futility of his flirtatious endeavor. 'I'm sorry, I'm not exactly skilled in the art of flirting.'

'But I am,' Firdaus responded with a playful grin. Aryan's heart raced, thundering louder than before as he absorbed her words. A million sentences formed in his mind, all vying to prolong the conversation. Yet, in the end, he managed to muster the courage to ask, 'Would you like to join me for a cup of coffee?'

'No,' she said sternly, rejecting his proposal.

'Why? He stammered. 'Did I say something wrong?' She smirked, 'No, but you look cute when you're nervous.' He shyly smiled.

'Are you up for grabbing a piping hot cup of masala chai instead of coffee?'

'At this hour.' He said, pointing at his wristwatch that showed 10 pm. 'This is Bombay. No one sleeps so early.' 'Fine, do you know a place?' 'I know the perfect place.'

Nariman Point was bustling with people walking, sitting, dancing, strolling, and doing all kinds of activities at 'this hour'. It was Aryan's first visit to Marine Drive. He was stunned by the gilded landscape. Along one side stretched the Arabian Sea, seeming darker than Satan's soul, while on the other side, Mumbai shimmered with a mesmerizing display of golden lights. 'These lights make this city brighter than it is.' Aryan thought, looking at the skyline. 'I know, this is my favourite spot. I often come here to ponder over my life and enjoy the tea.' Firdaus replied. Aryan smiled, and they kept walking.

'Want to sit?' She asked casually. 'Sure.' They motioned to the empty spot next to a snogging couple. 'This is so uncomfortable.' Aryan muttered. 'Don't look at them, and you'll be alright.' She suggested. 'How can you not look? They're right next to me.' 'Aryan, people here don't bother themselves with what others are doing, perhaps because we hardly pay attention to anyone besides ourselves. You'll get used to it, don't worry.' She said, tying her hair atop her head. 'Leave them loose.' Aryan said almost instinctively. She let her hair fall from the tight bun she had made half a second ago. Aryan lightly moved her hair strand from her face and placed it neatly behind her ears. 'We don't have to follow what these people are doing.' She pointed at the couple next to them tucked into each other's arms. Aryan quickly realized his action might have offended her, so he said, 'Sorry, I got carried away.' Firdaus blushed as he apologized. 'You're too gullible.'

Firdaus stopped the 'Chai Wala' who was yelling at the top of his voice, trying to grab people's attention to his stainless-steel tank that contained the world's best tea (according to him). 'Can I get two cups?' She asked and then grabbed her bag to take out her wallet. 'Let me pay.' Aryan offered. 'No, I got this. You can buy it next time.' Aryan felt relieved, thinking their outing was not that bad, and the girl had unknowingly stated that there was a chance they would meet again.

'Can I tell you something but promise me you won't tell anyone until it is safe to do so.' Firdaus wrapped her fingers around the hot cup and looked at Aryan. 'Yes, sure. What is it?' Aryan sat, crossed legs facing Firdaus.

'I feel there is more to Diamond Bazar than what meets the eyes.'

'What do you mean?' He asked, curling up his legs and moving them closer to his chest.

'I am trying to say that we have only recovered a fair bit of Nirvaan's treasure. There is surely more buried somewhere in his shop.'

'What makes you believe that?' Aryan asked solemnly, sliding into his rugged and skeptical personality, qualities most law enforcing officers harbour. 'We raided his house, properties and shops but found nothing other than retail products.'

'Don't you think a man like him would have kept something precious for himself?' Firdaus asked. 'If you confirm that he fled the country with nothing but his laptop, phone, and bag of clothes, then his treasure must still be here.'

'We have knocked down every wall in his house, snooped through all his left-over belongings and found no trace of anything besides what we have found in the shop.'

Firdaus had no proof. It was just her instinct or more of common sense. She remained silent until the salty breeze from the sea took over the tension she had unknowingly unleashed. Aryan felt responsible for shutting her down without giving her a chance to explain why she had those instincts. The uncomfortable silence between them made him anxious. He wanted to make her happy again, so he said, 'Fine. We'll go to the shop again and look at it with a fresh perspective. If we find something suspicious, I promise you, we'll dig deep.' Her wide smile melted his heart, and he felt like kissing her at that moment; he stopped himself somehow, thinking it would be inappropriate.

Firdaus and Aryan entered the two-storied shop after sunset the next day. They paced through the ground floor, checking the empty glass shelves (that once held precious gold and diamond jewellery), cabinets, cash counter and even the wooden flooring. Firdaus stomped her feet at two places that felt hollow from within, but to her dismay, there was no hidden locker underneath. It was just moisture build-up that made the wooden planks floatier. After repeatedly looking through empty spaces, Aryan finally asked the question he wanted to ask from the very beginning, 'what exactly are we looking for, Firdaus?'.

'I don't know, maybe a key to unlock his hidden treasure chest.' She replied.

'This is not a treasure hunt, Firdaus. We have thoroughly checked this place and gathered everything we could find.' He sighed.

'I would like to continue with my search. I'll understand if you wish to leave.' She flippantly shot back.

She led herself to the vast first floor that looked like an 18th-century library, only without books. The ostentatious carpeting, velvet curtains with gold tassels and floor-to-ceiling glass that overlooked a colonial building made the room appear straight out of a period drama. The first floor was built for VIP guests who demanded to see designer necklaces and one-of-a-kind jewels capable of explicitly adorning their necks and hands. Firdaus glanced through the walls that looked whiter at night, besides the portion that held beautiful paintings at once but now only displayed the dust gathered around the frame. 'There has to be something.' She murmured, gazing at the room.

The majestic carpet seemed washed and cleaned up and was smelling good as well, but it was curled up in one corner as if someone had tried to tear it. That tiny imperfection was so minor and hardly visible that it could have easily avoided attention, but Firdaus spotted it. She pulled it more with her hands. 'What are you doing?' Aryan followed her to the first floor. Firdaus held the corner of the carpet with one hand and slid the other underneath to look for a clue. Her moving fingers stumbled upon a key. Her eyes sparkled.

'Found it! See, I told you we will find something.' She cried out of excitement.

'What is it?' Aryan rushed to her.

'It's a key!'

Firdaus took the key and sped to Nirvaan's office. She turned on the lights and glanced through the room to look for the locker. His office was a mess. Drawers were emptied ruthlessly, stationary was thrown on the floor, glass paperweight was broken into pieces, and his fabric upholstered chair was torn from the middle. Carefully maneuvering through the room, Firdaus reached a wall-mounted shelf that held idols of Ganpati Ji and Lakshmi Ji (Indian gods believed to bring happiness and prosperity). She took the statues off the shelf and kept them on the table. Then, I pushed the shelf in. As the shelf motioned inwards, the wall panel that camouflaged the rest of the wall popped out. Firdaus touched the corners of the wall panel to find the lock; on the right-hand corner, she found the lock that accepted the key. 'Normally, most treasured jewels are believed to be guarded by god!' She explained. 'I knew from the moment I entered the office that if there was a locker, it had to be near the statue of the gods.' The wall panel finally uncloaked the locker, and they found the space filled with more jewellery, gold coins and bundles of cash. Firdaus rejoiced in her victory.

Aryan's mouth opened wide when he saw the treasure in the safe. 'Oh my god, you were right. This is a treasure! 'He got excited. She turned around and hugged him, leaving him flustered and tongue-tied. He gradually wrapped his arms around her and said, 'Firdaus, you are our own Indiana Jones.'

Hearing that, she tilted her head and kissed him on his cheek. 'India Jones is better than Fifi. I approve of this name. 'She blushed.

Aryan's heart throbbed so intensely that he felt it would tear out his chest. No one had ever kissed him so gently, and there he was, standing next to the love of his life who had done something he had only dreamt of. 'We should celebrate.' She suggested.

'Ye-yes,' He stammered.

'Oh, Aryan, for once, be confident.' She muttered. 'I'll get the champagne.'

'And I'll inform the CBI to come and collect this first thing in the morning.'

'Please, Aryan, you can do that later. Let us first drink and dance to our victory.' She held his hand and dragged him out of the store. 'Trust me, nothing is going to happen to that locker. It's anyway too late to call your supervisor. The first thing Dhimant would say is, 'why did you visit the store without my permission.' She was correct; he had no idea how his boss would react. His loud breathing reflected the hundreds of ifs and buts suffocating his head.

'But Firdaus, I have to inform them.'

'Your hysterics are making me nervous. Don't overthink this; let us go somewhere and celebrate.' She insisted.

'Alright, let's go to my place.' Said Aryan.

'Perfect, I'll get the champagne on the way.'

Aryan's 2nd-floor apartment was small yet cosy. It was scarcely furnished, just a couch under the window and a chair adjacent to it. 'Sorry, I recently moved to Mumbai, so I have not got the time to shop for furniture.' He said anxiously, organizing the cushions on the couch.

'Don't worry, I am comfortable.'

'Do you want tea?' He asked nervously.

Firdaus pointed at the bottle of champagne she was carrying and said, 'why did I bring this if we wanted to drink tea?'

'Oh yes, you're right.' Aryan replied sheepishly.

Noticing his perpetual nervousness around her, she realized he never had a woman's company in his apartment. 'Do you have candles?' She asked candidly.

'Yes, I do.' He replied, grabbing the candle he had placed on the kitchen platform.

'I am surprised you own a candle.'

'Well, to be honest, this one's not for aesthetics. It saves me from bumping into things when the electricity is gone.'

'Oh, I see. Now, let's celebrate. Shall we?' And saying that, Firdaus popped open the champagne. Poured it into two tea mugs (as

Aryan's crockery collection had nothing more than two plates, two bowls and two mugs.)

Aryan connected his phone to a portable speaker he had carried along with a few clothes he brought from Delhi and played his favourite classics. After finishing half a bottle of champagne in half an hour, they hogged out on instant noodles. They danced to their favourite song, 'falling in love with you' which melodiously played in the background.

The moon shone brightly as the night progressed and beamed through the window, making the couple's eyes twinkle. Firdaus moved her body closer and wrapped her arms around his neck. He couldn't stop staring at her beautiful face that looked more radiant in the moonlight and her lean body that lightly moved to the song's melody. He wrapped his arm around her torso and pulled her closer. 'I bet you'll need more champagne to kiss me.' She said teasingly. He picked up the bottle and gulped a few sips, 'You're right, darling!'.

After consuming a full bottle of Champagne, the couple were into each other's arms. Aryan surprised Firdaus by kissing her, and when she kissed him back, Aryan finally got the confidence to take her to the bedroom.

* * *

Firdaus's phone beeped at 4 am, notifying her of the text she had received. Rubbing her drowsy eyes, she took the phone and read the text. Firdaus got off the bed and sneaked out of the room, ensuring Aryan was still asleep. She opened her Uber app, typed her destination - 'Diamond Bazar, Nariman point' and pressed the 'Order' button.

In fifteen minutes, she reached the shop where two men in black leather jackets were waiting for her. 'You're late, Firdaus. Now make it fast.' Said one of the men.

'You both stay here. Let me go up and get it.' Firdaus opened the lock with the keys she had sneaked into her bag when Aryan was fast asleep. She strode to Nirvaan's office and took out all the money and jewellery they had found in his locker. She threw them all in the black bag the men had brought along. She locked the safe and got out of the shop. 'Here, take it.' She told the men, handing them the bag. 'I want my money now.'

'Boss has sent a generous advance, and the rest will be given to you once we sell everything in the black market.' One man gestured to the other to take out the envelope their boss had given them. The other man took out the envelope from his back pocket and gave it to Firdaus. 'Khudahafiz,' the men said, bidding her farewell. Firdaus dropped the envelope in her tote bag and took a rickshaw back home.

Suddenly, Aryan cried, 'Firdaus, you betrayed me! I hate you. You're a thief. You used me for your own benefit.'

Firdaus flinched and woke up. Her head was still leaning on the car's window when she realized she had been dreaming of her past.

'What happened, Firdaus? Are you okay?' Aryan asked.

'Yes, I am fine. Don't know when I fell asleep.'

'It's okay. We still have two hours before we reach Udaipur. Go back to sleep if you're tired.' Firdaus's heart sank watching him next to her. She wiped her face with a small hand towel she was carrying in her bag and sulked in the guilt that had dreaded her heart for long.

She had to divert her mind to snap out of the guilt that was choking her, so she started reading 'Filthy Rich Royals,' the book Ms DeMello gave her before leaving.

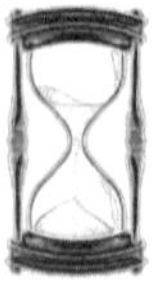

Chapter 7

Fateh Prakash Palace, Udaipur

An elaborate luncheon was organized for the royalty of Patiala, who was to visit the city of Udaipur that afternoon. The gathering was meant to happen in the Royal Durbar Hall. It was the largest and most luxurious banquet in the hotel. The Durbar Hall held larger-than-life chandeliers, dynasty-owned weapons shielded by thick glass, exquisite paintings and relics that displayed the rich heritage of Mewar. Large circular tables were embellished with flower vases, brass plates, champagne glasses, and finest cutleries to impress the guests. The chairs around were bejewelled with satin ribbons and soft cushions, offering a plethora of comfort and luxury.

Ajit Singh, the enigmatic majority owner of the illustrious establishment that was Fateh Prakash Palace Hotel, would usually visit once every quarter to scrutinize the meticulous workings of managerial and financial administration of the hotel. Upon this particular occasion, anticipation stirred the corridors of the hotel and people murmured in hushed voices that Singh was probably not going to arrive alone. He was believed to approach with an entourage of potential foreign investors keen to infuse capital into his ventures. However, the gossip was that these investors were not invited to invest capital. Instead, they were prompted to rescue Singh from bankruptcy by acquiring some of his properties.

Aryan and Firdaus had arrived at the palace hotel a little early and were waiting in the lobby. To avoid attention, Firdaus was pretending to discuss the itinerary for the day with Aryan, but all her attention was on the gossip circulating the palace. Hearing the news of his bankruptcy, she thought that they had a better chance at convincing the Prince's nephew not to tell them but sell them the location of the necklace. She casually glanced around the lobby to see if Ajit had arrived. 'You think Mr Singh will help us?' Aryan murmured, covering his mouth with the brochure. 'I don't know. Maybe not, but we must try our luck.' She replied.

The anxious manager was yelling at the staff for not double-checking the preparations. All the cutleries should have been made of silver and not steel; that was his order. There were a couple steel spoons on a table that boiled his blood. His voice was heard through the corridor till the lobby. The perfection expected had to be achieved before Ajit Singh's arrival.

All the guests were being escorted to the Durbar Hall. The hotel staff stood at the entrance to welcome their esteemed invitees by showering rose petals on them as they walked through the corridor. They offered rose water to wash their hands and warm hand towels to wipe them clean as they entered the hall. When all the guests settled in, an announcement was made informing everyone that Mr Ajit Singh had arrived and would join everyone in the next half an hour.

A gamut of cuisines prepared for the luncheon oozed a tantalizing aroma that made Aryan hungry. He wondered if they had eaten at all in the past few days. 'The smell of the food is making my mouth water.' He grunted. 'Shhh, keep quiet. We're not here to eat, and we are not even invited. Let us just focus on meeting this Ajit guy before he comes to the luncheon. I don't want him to be distracted when we ask him about the Patiala necklace.'

They walked up to the reception and asked the receptionist if Ajit Singh had arrived. Not being too obvious with the question, Firdaus asked, 'I have heard the prince of Patiala is staying here. Is that right?'

'Yes, mam, are you a guest invited to the luncheon?' The receptionist asked.

'Do we look like people invited to such an event?' Mihir spoke in Firdaus's ear.

Firdaus didn't react and kept talking to the receptionist. 'Yes, we are. But I was wondering if I could see him before the event. I need to discuss something really important.'

'We can't allow that, madam. His security is our priority. Sorry,' The face of the receptionist was as stiff as a marble.

'Actually, the thing is…' Firdaus prattled for a bit and then said, 'he might be expecting us.' The receptionist still had the same expressions. 'Sorry ma'am, I can't help you. If you have an appointment, you'll have to speak with her.' She pointed at a lady standing near the lift.

Firdaus walked up to her and said, 'ma'am, I am Firdaus; I am here to meet Mr. Ajit Singh.' The lady, who must be his manager, turned around. She gave her an acerbic look. 'Wait here.' She said sharply, then got into the lift and ascended to the top floor.

'What the hell is going on?' Aryan asked anxiously.

'I don't know; we will find out soon, though.'

In five minutes, the manager came down and escorted Firdaus and Aryan to the 14th floor. She was quiet throughout their way to the top floor and then when they got off the lift, she informed them that Singh was late for the luncheon and would only give them five minutes of his time. Her tone was mechanical, almost like a recorded machine.

'How did you succeed in blackmailing Mrs Desai? I forgot to ask you.' Aryan whispered, but before Firdaus could reply, he smugly said, 'Well, why am I even asking? It's you, blackmailing, stealing, lying. All these are your inherent traits.'

Firdaus winced and kept her pace. The manager ushered them to the VIP suite, which had a Master-bedroom hosting a majestic king-size bed, a living room with a huge sofa adorned with traditional cushions, a 50-inch LED TV, a fully loaded bar and a breezy balcony overlooking Lake Pichola. The VIP suite was nothing short of an oasis of luxury. Amazed by the interior, Aryan lowered his speed to look around the room. In contrast, Firdaus strode straight to Singh. He was drinking tea sitting on the balcony.

Firdaus had come prepared to blackmail Singh if he refused to comply. Coming straight to the point, she asked him about the Patiala Necklace and its current location. Ajit replied placidly, 'it vanished from our treasury years ago, and I don't know where it has been ever since.' A harmless answer like such was expected out of him, so Firdaus countered, 'a family heirloom so precious is gone, and none of you bothered to look for it. I don't believe that.'

'You can choose to believe whatever you want.' He snapped.

'Listen, Firdaus was straightforward. If you tell us where the necklace is, we'll pay you. Big time,' she said with a hint of nonchalance.

Ajit chuckled 'Are you for real? You're asking me to reveal the whereabouts of the necklace for money? Have you forgotten that it's my family's heirloom? If money was the issue, I'd sell the necklace itself and not its location. I'm pretty sure selling the Patiala Necklace would fetch me way more than selling out its hiding place.'

'Sir, you'll have to comply with us with all due respect. I am an ASI officer, and I have the legal right to interrogate you regarding the disappearance of the necklace.' Aryan intervened.

'And yet you had to blackmail Mrinalini for this rendezvous.' he ridiculed.

The two kept quiet, resenting the tactic they had used to harass Mrs Desai and now Mr Singh. 'Some call you a relic hunter and some a black-market dealer, but officially, you're just a librarian.' He paused to look for a reaction and then continued, 'Whoever you're Ms or you young man, I am not going to give you any information about the necklace. Even if I had known where it was, I would not share it with anyone. Now, if we're done here, I want to join my guests at the luncheon.'

'Firdaus, please pull out an ace. Now is the time.' Aryan thought.

But Firdaus just smiled, thanked Singh for his time and gestured for Aryan to leave him alone.

'I know you're curious as to why I just got up and left.' 'Yes, out of all other times, you choose now to keep your mouth shut. I can't believe you screwed this up.'

'Relax, Aryan, there is no point pushing him when I know where the Patiala Necklace is.' She whispered.

Before entering Ajit's suite, I had received a text from Black Jack saying the Necklace is at the Illuminati Art Gallery, Udaipur. She explained. I didn't believe my eyes when I first read the message, but I trust Black Jack. His information is always authentic.'

'So, we found it. That's it?' Aryan curiously asked.

'Yes, I think so.' She replied.

* * *

Wearing a crisp white shirt, black pants, and a blazer, Aryan stood in the hotel foyer waiting for Firdaus. He gazed at the beautiful two-tiered Victorian-style fountain at the entrance that dramatically discharged water that somehow soothed his jittery nerves. Sensing a flux of familiar scent, he turned around to look for the source. He found Firdaus walking towards him in a red body-hugging satin evening gown wearing the same perfume that had enticed him five years ago. With her hair tied in a bun atop her head and a face glowing with the makeup she applied, Firdaus looked ravishing. Aryan offered his hand to escort her. She laid her hand in the crook of his elbow as he walked her to the car and chivalrously opened the door for her to get in.

'Well, chivalry is not dead.' She murmured.

'Did you say something?' Aryan asked, locking his gaze into her eyes. She nodded. 'Firdaus you...' he paused, 'Yes, I what?' 'You look… hmm.' 'Beautiful, is that the word you're looking for?' She teased him.

'Yes, you're gorgeous.' He uttered and then turned his eyes towards the road, trying to stop himself from falling in love again.

'Why can't I hate her?' He asked himself. After all, she has done everything to ruin my career and break my trust, then why do I fall for her pretence every time I see her? He scratched his forehead in frustration. 'Are you okay?' She asked. 'I feel like I need a drink.' Firdaus laughed, 'I hope you've worked on your capacity in all these years.' Well, Gin & Tonic has been my friend in adversity. I have relied on it too often to be my support in pain. Firdaus sighed. 'Come on, don't over-exaggerate your alcoholism. I have seen you sober all these days. That is true. Aryan thought. Maybe that could be the reason to convince myself not to hate her. Since working with her, he hasn't felt the compulsive need to drink, which he often felt before.

The gallery exhibited one-of-a-kind jewels from around the world. Cartier's boastful creation, The Patiala Necklace, was placed at the centre and was surrounded by curious eyes trying to embrace the beauty of the masterpiece. Firdaus handed her invitation (she had managed to obtain it from a guest who fell for her pretentious flirting) to the guard, who not-so-politely told everyone, 'This event is invitation only. Please show your invite or kindly step out of the line.'

Firdaus was enchanted by the elaborate display of artifacts and jewels at the exhibition and thought they would cost millions in the black market. However, she strode straight to the Patiala necklace without wasting much time marvelling through the gallery (which she would have done under any other circumstances).

Aryan and Firdaus caught a glimpse of the Patiala Necklace standing in the crowd surrounding the jewel. The Necklace was displayed on a black velvet easel and looked extravagant from the glass that shielded it. Firdaus walked closer to the display to read the plaque underneath. 'This is only a replica of the original Patiala Necklace.' She read the paragraph that followed. Our craftsmen have tried to recreate the design of the Patiala necklace initially made by the house of Cartier in 1928 for Prince Amrendra Singh. All the stones used in this necklace are engineered and not real.'

Aryan started laughing hysterically, reading the plaque and clapped frantically with his face turned towards Firdaus. His obscurity made him the centre of many frowning eyes and scowling faces. 'What are you doing? Have you lost it?' Yelled Firdaus.

'No, I am just laughing at you. You forced and blackmailed people, even bribed some to find the necklace and look where it led you.' She came forth and held his hand, 'Aryan, let it go.' 'There is no need to make a scene.' She muttered. He unclasped his hand from hers and threw it in the air, 'ladies and gentlemen, may I have your attention? I would like to raise a toast to my friend here who paid twenty-lakhs to a man to find the Patiala necklace, only to realize she could have found it for free through the internet.' Hushed murmurs and audible smirks came through the crowd, making Firdaus even more uncomfortable. Aryan stopped the waiter who was serving refreshments to the guests, took a glass of whisky from his tray and swallowed the drink in one sip.

'Everybody, she deserves a big applause, doesn't she? He shouted. Having had enough of his drama, one of the guests went to the guard and asked him to escort the man out as soon as possible. Firdaus was already resentful of her failure, and Aryan's jibe had worsened her mood. Unable to handle more embarrassment, she stormed out of the gallery and brisked to the nearest alleyway. She kept her pace and traversed from one alley to another. The light from the streetlamps gradually faded as she walked deeper into some neighbourhood that appeared more like a rendezvous spot for dodgy dealings.

Not many people were out on the streets, only a few unscrupulous ones who were talking in whispers and ogling at her beautiful legs that stretched out of the slit of her dress.

After walking for half a kilometre, Firdaus reached a wrecking yard where many broken cars were parked. 'What fresh hell is this?' She wondered, looking at vehicles stacked on top of one another. 'Damn, I am lost.' Firdaus turned on her phone and opened Google Maps to search for her location. The map showed that she was about ten kilometres away from the hotel. She followed the directions shown on the app and started walking back to the hotel. After walking for a bit, she heard a car passing through and thought of asking for a lift. The driver stopped the car, watching her coming towards them, and rolled down the window to talk to her. When Firdaus saw who the driver was, she froze out of panic. It was the same man who stood outside the Diamond Bazaar five years ago.

'Firdaus Durrani.' A sombre voice called her from the car. Her heart raced when she saw three men in the car and realized she was alone and in danger. To save herself, she ran. The driver and the other three men followed her. 'She should not get away this time. Let us catch her.' The driver ordered the rest.

'Yes, boss. She'll not get away.' The men roared and ran after her. Hiding from those men, Firdaus ran into Aryan, who had come looking for her.

'Why are you running?' He asked. 'I'll explain later. Just come with me.' She held his hand and paced towards the main road. One of the men came through the side lane and caught her by her waist. He pushed Aryan away and dragged Firdaus to the side. 'You bitch, where is our money?' He asked, pressing his hand against her neck. She wheezed, trying to breathe. 'Leave me. I'll pay you back.' She pleaded. Aryan punched the assailant with a balled fist, making him fall to the ground and ran to Firdaus to see if she was okay. 'I am fine, Aryan.' 'Are you hurt? He asked with concern. Firdaus's eyes widened as she yelled, 'Watch out.'

The driver hit his head with a brick, making him drop unconscious on the ground. 'Oh god, Aryan.' Firdaus cried, watching blood dripping from behind his ears. The driver then grasped her hand, twisted it as she swung, and recoiled in pain. To break free, she kicked him in the groin with her pointy stilettos, making him tremble in pain and then fall. The other two men gave her a death stare, standing across from her, and yelled, 'You give our money back, and we will let you go.'

Firdaus breathed rapidly out of fear and exhaustion. She saw some stones on the gravel, so she picked them up and threw them at them. They managed to dodge the attack, and finally, tired of the scuffle, one of them took out a gun from behind his back and pointed it straight toward Firdaus.

'You think you're a smart woman? You can betray us and take our money without any consequences?' Firdaus raised both her hands, gesturing her surrender. 'I'll pay you back, believe me. My friend is injured. Let me take him to the hospital first. I promise I'll give everything I owe.' The man walked closer to her and placed the gunpoint on her forehead. 'You're a liar. You have lied enough, but not anymore.' He was just about to press the trigger when a bullet hit his skull, dropping him dead on the ground.

Another shot came through, injuring the other man's leg. Watching him distracted with his wound, Firdaus snapped the gun from the dead man's hand and pointed it at the bruised-eyed man coming for her. 'Leave before I shoot you.' She said ferociously. The intensely wounded and petrified men ran to their car and drove off.

Firdaus hastened to attend to Aryan and placed his head over her lap. 'Aryan, please wake up.' She cupped his face into her hands and shook it several times to get him to consciousness. When his body did not respond, she cried for help. Listening to her alarming voice, a man in the blue suit came to aid. He hovered his finger below his nostrils to check if he was still breathing and then placed his hand on his wrist to check for a pulse. 'He is breathing normally. There is nothing to worry about. He'll hopefully come to consciousness soon.' He declared.

'Are you a doctor?'

'No, but I can tell with certainty that he is fine. However, for peace of mind, you can take him to the hospital at dawn. For now, let us take him back to the hotel.' He suggested.

When Firdaus seemed convinced, he picked him up from the ground, resting one of his arms on his shoulder and the other on Firdaus and took him to the car.

When they reached the hotel, he brought Aryan to his room and laid him on the bed. 'Thank you for your help.' Firdaus offered her gratitude to the gentleman. 'No problem.' He smiled. 'Was it you who shot the men?' She asked nervously. 'I saw a helpless woman kneeling at gunpoint, and I couldn't stop myself from helping her.' 'I don't know how to thank you. You killed a man and injured another for two people you barely know.' She said sheepishly. 'Don't think about them anymore. They're gone, and I am glad you two are safe.'

She smiled and asked for his introduction. 'I forgot to ask your name?' 'I am Sidharth Singh.' He offered a handshake.

'I am Firdaus Durrani. Nice to meet you!'

Repeating his name, Firdaus wondered, 'any connection to Ajit Singh, prince of Patiala?' He laughed briefly and replied, 'Yes, he is my father.'

Aryan moaned in pain. 'Uff...my head hurts. He whimpered. 'Aryan, you should rest. You're hurt.' Firdaus gave him a glass of water to drink. 'Have this and then go to sleep.' Shockingly staring at the blue suit, he asked, 'What are you doing here?' Sidharth came closer to the bed and introduced himself, 'Hi, I am Sidharth Singh.' 'He is Ajit Singh's son. He found us on the street and was kind enough to help.' Firdaus interrupted. Looking at Aryan's awful state and Firdaus's fatigued face, he said, 'you two should rest tonight.'

Firdaus escorted him to the door as he prepared to leave, but then he suddenly swung around and asked Firdaus if they both could join him for breakfast tomorrow. She immediately accepted his invitation and wished him a good night as he exited the room.

Firdaus told Aryan that she would stay the night in his room to look after him should there be a need. She took the couch to avoid any conflict and settled there while Aryan used the bathroom.

'Do you want a t-shirt? I am sure you don't want to sleep in that half-torn muddy dress.' Aryan threw a curled t-shirt from his bag toward Firdaus.

'Thanks. If you don't need the bathroom, can I use it?' She asked.

'Yes, sure, go ahead.' He replied.

As soon as she entered the bathroom to shower, Aryan swiftly sneaked out of the room and went to room number 607. He knocked on the door and whispered, 'It's me. Open the door.' Sidharth opened the door and dragged him in.

'What are you doing here, and why are you posing as Sidharth Singh?' 'I can't tell you anything; it's against the protocol.' He stated stoically. 'What have I gotten into.' Aryan sighed, dropping himself on the bed.

'Listen, Aryan, I know you have many questions. Believe me, I'll tell you everything in time, but I want you to play along so I can stop Firdaus from finding that necklace.'

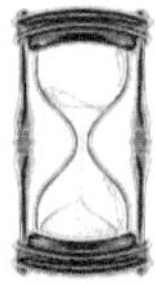

Chapter 8

Fateh Prakash Palace, Udaipur

Aryan's head was hurting and his patience to deal with everything going on around him was thinning with time. Firdaus was all dressed up to attend the breakfast and was waiting for Aryan to accompany her.

'Can you please hurry up?' She exasperated.

I am trying my best, Firdaus. Aryan tried to be polite despite the situation.

'I am positive, we'll most definitely find a clue from this man.' Firdaus stated positively.

Aryan clasped his leather belt and turned around to face Firdaus. 'Do you realise how much trouble we all are in? You still haven't told me why finding this necklace is important to you, so much so that you're mercilessly pursuing every lead possible without thinking about how perilous that can turn out to be.

'Aryan, just breathe.' Firdaus sensed the tension in his voice.

'I know this is tough. Yesterday, you got hurt because of me.'

'Hurt? You mean almost killed.'

'Can you please calm down? Trust me, I'll tell you everything when the time is right.' Firdaus said in a pleading voice.

'You keep saying that, but it's hard for me to trust you. I wish I would have denied going on this expedition with you.'

'I wish that too.' Whispered Firdaus.

The breakfast buffet was set on the balcony in Sidharth's room, which was smaller and less luxurious than his so-called father's suite. The balcony overlooked the lush gardens adorned with manicured shrubs, healthy green grass, a couple of gazebos and a row of frangipani trees tall enough to shroud the place's magnificence from the outside world. Sidharth had ordered continental breakfast for his guests, and the serving crew had placed the breakfast items in the order of their consumption. Juice, coffee, tea, and assorted bread on the left, then cereal, muffins, fresh fruits and egg items on the right.

Firdaus and Aryan filled their plates and settled beside Sidharth on the table. 'Good morning, how are you feeling now?' He asked them both. 'Much better now. Thanks again for helping us yesterday and inviting us to breakfast this morning.' She replied, and Aryan nodded along. Sidharth emptied the sugar-free packet into his black coffee and stirred it well before taking a sip. 'It's my pleasure to have your company.' He said. The three of them then ate their breakfast in silence before Sidharth finally revealed the reason for his invitation.

'Pardon me for being direct, but honestly, my agenda for inviting you guys to breakfast is to discuss your search for the Patiala necklace.' He said, wiping his mouth with the hand towel placed next to his plate. Seeming prepared for this conversation, Firdaus replied, 'I know this already.' Aryan choked on a piece of sweet melon while listening to the conversation, pretending to play along when he clearly sucked at both lying and acting. Firdaus pushed a glass of water towards him, spilling a little on the way. 'Have this.' She said sternly.

'Mr Singh, you introduced yourself as the son of Prince Ajit Singh, but as per my research, he has only one son, and he is 10 years old.'

Sidharth smirked at her insinuation and replied, 'you're right. He only has one legitimate son who is also my half-brother.' I introduced myself as Sidharth Singh to you, but I generally go by Sidharth Desai.

Firdaus's eyes widened at his revelation. 'Yes, I am Mrs Mrinalini Desai's son and a bastard of Prince Ajit Singh.'

Aryan swallowed the whole glass of water and stomped it on the table. 'Are you alright, Mr Verma?' Sidharth asked.

'Yes. I am fine.' He stammered.

Sidharth's deep grey eyes gazed at Aryan, gesturing him to pull himself together.

'What makes you so interested in our hunt for the Necklace?

'Oh no, you got me all wrong. I don't want any information from you. I have called you here to give you a clue that might aid your search.'

'And why would you do that?'

'Because our destination is the same, and we are walking on different paths. But if we flock, we'll get there sooner. So, what do you say, are you in?'

'I don't believe you, but I want to find that necklace at any cost.'

'As do I.'

'Let us share our strengths and find the necklace together, then we will decide who gets it. Deal?

'Depends on your information and how important it is.' Firdaus kept her gaze intact.

'Well played, Firdaus, so here it is. When I was young, my father would visit me rarely, but when he would, he would tell me a story. A story of a doomed treasure that a giant snake swallowed. The treasure rested in his stomach and exuded its evil powers, making the snake delirious over time. To save everyone in the village, the sarpanch hunted it down, locked him in a dungeon, and then declared that everyone would always remain safe until the snake and treasure were locked in.'

'I might have something that would decode the context behind this story.' Firdaus declared in excitement.

'And I am sure a talented person like yourself will decode it soon.'

Firdaus rushed to her room, grabbed the book Ms DeMello had given her and quickly flipped through some pages, reaching a section about the royal family of Thiruvananthapuram. She read loudly; the *mystery of the treasure of the Padmanabhaswamy temple is shrouded more in fear than curiosity. The legend has it that anyone who opens the vault and disturbs the cobras rumoured to protect the treasure will be met with a catastrophe worse enough to doom not only the finder but their loved ones too. While the other vaults have been opened, unveiling priceless artifacts and gold, vault B remains closed and continues to frighten the localities.*

'So, this is where the necklace is.' She thought, then pulled her laptop out of her bag and turned it on. She typed two words, Anand Krishnamurthy and Padmanabhaswamy Temple. The internet pulled up a few articles from the archives that contained information on the Krishnamurthy family and their connection to Padmanabhaswamy Temple. She clicked on various articles and glanced through them, trying to look for a relationship between his family and the royal family of Patiala.

Anand Krishnamurthy belonged to the royal blood, but his forefathers had pledged to be the vassals of the temple. They have served as 'Dasa' and 'Sevenis' of the temple ever since. After rigorously going through tons of links, Firdaus stumbled upon an old newspaper clipping that displayed the photo of Mr Krishnamurthy's father with Prince Amrendra Singh. Firdaus jumped off her seat out of nervous excitement. She rubbed her hand across her face and jolted in excitement. 'Don't get ahead of yourself, Firdaus. Though Sidharth's cryptic story matches the description of the vault, and the longstanding friendship between the Singhs and the Krishnamurthy family adds to the evidence, all this could be coincidental or circumstantial.' She told herself.

'What the hell are you doing?' Aryan yelled as soon as Firdaus left.

'Can you keep your voice low?'

'You told me you wanted to stop her from finding the necklace, then why did you give her that clue?' Aryan fired back.

'I am only following orders.' He responded placidly.

Aryan ran his fingers through his hair and held them back tightly. 'I am going crazy. You all are lying, and I am left to choose which lie to believe.'

'I would ask you to believe me, but I know you won't.'

'Tell me what's going on before I lose my mind. Please, my friend.'

'You need to follow Firdaus and do as she says. Trust me, it'll all make sense in the end.'

Aryan stared at him in disgust and then left the room in range.

He followed Firdaus to her room and found her pacing through the space ecstatically. 'What is going on, Firdaus? Are you okay?'

'I have found the location of the necklace.' Aryan's eyes sparkled with excitement. 'Was Sidharth's story helpful?'

'Yes, it cleared up everything. Now the whole story adds up.' 'The Patiala necklace, although extremely precious, only brought misery to the royal family of Patiala. The king lost his love, falling prey to the luring crown, and the prince lost his pride, courage, and will to live and eventually committed suicide. They blamed the necklace for the death of their rulers and the misfortune that followed. Perhaps to save the family from further mishaps, they locked away the necklace with the help of Krishnamurthy family.

'Who are the Krishnamurthys?' Aryan asked curiously.

'I'll tell you everything on the way. We have to go to Kerala.'

'What about Sidharth?'

'What about him?'

'We'll not let him know. Simple.'

'Firdaus, he helped us for his own cause.'

'Exactly.'

'I have my doubts about him, but I don't have the time to investigate it. Whoever he is, or if he is really after the necklace as he says, then we must hurry and reach Kerala before he does.'

Aryan sent a text to Sidharth informing him of their plan to go to Thiruvananthapuram before boarding the flight. He was skeptical of his action, but he did what he felt was right at that moment.

He sat upright and relatively formally on his seat, pretending to read a magazine. Firdaus clung to her laptop to research the temple's history, the custodians and underground vaults holding alleged wealth and treasure. '

What are you doing, Firdaus?' He asked, finally tired of fidgeting with everything in proximity and drinking carelessly out of anxiety.

'Can't you see I am researching? We need to be prepared.'

'Prepared for what? He asked.

She glanced at him, 'are you stupid, or have you been drinking a lot? She exasperated.

'No, I am fine. 'I just don't know what you're up to.' And don't call me stupid.' He looked disturbed.

'You don't involve me in your plan. All you do is give commands, Aryan do this, Aryan come with me.' He said, imitating her. 'Listen to me carefully. Pull yourself together. You have been acting weirdly since this morning. 'Don't act foolishly, especially now. We're so close, Aryan. If I get the necklace, all our troubles will end.

'First of all, tell me what your troubles are', He slurred while speaking. Regretting what had slipped out of her tongue, she said, 'nothing, there is no trouble.' 'Don't lie. I know something is troubling you. You're clearly sad, and I can't see you like this. You know I love you.' He held her hand, taking her by surprise.

'I want to tell you something, Firdaus.'

'Yes, what is it?' Her mouth went dry.

'My life has always been boring. I have no dreams, no passion, no love, nothing. But whenever you come into my life, you bring adventure. Do you know what I fear the most? He asked, bringing his face near to hers. 'Getting out of my comfort zone. I hate doing anything that's not on the list. I like things planned. I have always, most naturally, liked security and comfort, but with you, I feel free, like a bird flying in the vast sky.'

Firdaus felt the urge to tell him the truth, but she chose to maintain her composure and focus on the matter. Aryan slid his arm into her arm and kept his head on her shoulder. 'I guess I should sleep now.' He announced. 'Oh, Aryan!' She sighed.

As the flight landed, Firdaus walked up to the first coffee stall she could spot at the airport and bought two cups of coffee. 'Here, this will help you.' She said, handing him his cup.

'My head hurts. I need more caffeine to recoup.' He said, rubbing his eyes and face.

She lit her cigarette and offered the packet to Aryan. Aryan kept looking at her in surprise. 'I haven't seen you smoke in a while.'

Don't tell me you quit smoking. I did a few years ago. Well, if you want to get back to it, I don't see a more suitable time than this.' She said flippantly.

He pulled a cigarette from the packet and inhaled a drag. 'Oh, Firdaus, you always make me do things I later regret.'

'Finally, it looks like you're sobering up.'

'How can you tell?'

'Under intoxication, you happen to like me.'

'I like you otherwise also.' Aryan smiled.

'Really, well, that's a change. I thought I was topping the list of your most hated people.'

'You know that's not true. It's just that you lie easily and I am unable to figure out when you're lying and when you aren't.'

'Aryan, you don't have to trust me this time. All you need to know is that this is important to me.'

Aryan waited for her to say more, explain her situation better, but she didn't and as usual he nodded, being sympathetic to her conundrum.

* * *

They entered the temple from a monumental gate, also known as gopuram. The pale granite facade etched with ornate images of gods displayed the excellence of an architectural marvel hardly seen elsewhere other than in the south of India. Firdaus stood stunned, looking at the window-like openings in the centre of the pyramidal structure aligned vertically from the bottom to the top of the gopuram. At the top of the edifice was a set of evenly spaced seven Kalasha. She heard the group of worshipers telling each other stories about the rare visual, which is more of a spectacle that unfolds twice a year on the day of the equinox. 'One gets to see the setting sun passing through all the windows in the gopuram in succession in five-minute intervals.' The tour guide accompanying the group announced.

'Isn't that cool'? Aryan asked, hearing the tour guide's commentary.

'The beauty of this temple is beyond my imagination. 'She declared, standing mesmerised. 'Do you want to visit the sanctum? 'I would love to, but right now, we have to spread out and look for the place that leads us to the vaults. You cover the interior, take pictures of unusual places, and I'll cover the exterior. We'll meet here in half an hour. They decided.

The deity of Lord Vishnu was enshrined in a supine position with five snakes inclined towards him, guarding him for eternity. The space around the sanctum sanctorum was filled with devotees and worshipers chanting prayers in various languages. Aryan looked around and took out his phone to click pictures. When he turned on the camera, he saw the board that said photography was prohibited inside the temple. He kept his phone back in his pocket and strolled around with other worshipers to pass the time.

Firdaus, on the other hand, hellbent on finding the chamber, stooped every time she walked past the sewer opening. She sneaked into the administrative office and tried manipulating the manager to get information on vault B. 'I hear many stories of the temple treasure. Is any of that true?' She asked the bookkeeper.

'No, madam, people love to make stories, but there is hardly any truth to it.'

'Not all what people say is fiction. There must be some truth to it. I have come from very far, and I can't go back before exploring the temple. How about you show me around?' She proposed.

'I am just a bookkeeper, but if you want to look around, I can organise a guided tour.' Realizing that her charm was not working on the poor guy, she left him alone. 'Oh, there is no need for that. I'll take your leave now.'

Losing her patience, she walked through the temple hysterically, looking for a hidden door, a crypt or an ancient wall covered in dust and webs. 'What are you looking for, young lady?' A solemn voice came from behind. Firdaus turned around and saw a half-naked man wrapped in a delicate white loincloth. His swarthy face, covered in wrinkles, suggested he was in his early sixties. 'I am…a..a…a' she gulped her saliva twice, trying to finish the sentence. 'I know you're here for the treasure. I can tell because I know your kind.' Said the priest. 'I wouldn't deny there is no treasure; there is a lot, but all of that belongs to the lord.'

'I don't want the treasure. I just want the Patiala necklace.' Firdaus replied truthfully.

'Everything in this temple belongs to our God, and no one has ever succeeded in taking anything that belongs to the Almighty.

'I need the necklace, and I must get it.' She said vehemently.

I'll give you the exact location of the vault your necklace is in and the best time to take it out, but I challenge you, you won't succeed in your endeavours. He paused and then continued, however, if you prove me wrong, I'll personally escort you through the security and allow you to take whatever you have stolen.'

'If you want to know where the vaults are, follow me.' Said he. They walked into the temple and circled the pious deity of Lord Vishnu. 'At dawn tomorrow, we will be removing this idol from the sanctum sanctorum and parade it around the courtyard. You're lucky as this festivity rarely occurs around here, and tomorrow is that rare occasion. Vault B is located underneath the idol, and when the idol is removed, you'll have access to the vault.' Said the swarthy-faced priest. 'I am sure you won't be able to open the vault, but I still wish you the best of luck.

'May God help you.' He smirked.

'He will. He has to.' She murmured.

'Who are you, if I may ask?' She asked, lowering her voice.

'I am the caretaker of this temple, and my name is Anand Krishnamurthy.'

Aryan joined Firdaus and the priest after extensively strolling through the internal and external premises of the temple. 'I was looking for you everywhere.' He said, gasping for a breath. He introduced himself to the priest and complimented him for taking good care of the temple. 'I don't think there is any treasure here. I checked everything but found nothing suspicious. We must leave now.' He whispered in her ear. 'No problem, Aryan, let's go. I have gotten all the information I needed.' She said, fixing her gaze at the priest. 'I am glad I was able to help you.' He replied.

On their way to the hotel, Aryan asked Firdaus if she had found the treasure's location. She told him she knew where the necklace was and suggested planning to get it out of the vault at dawn. 'So that priest told you where the necklace is. I can't believe he gave away a big secret so easily.' Aryan uttered in disbelief.

'Like a true believer, he thinks the curse is real, and we won't succeed in getting the necklace out of the vault. The ill-omen will destroy us even before we try.' She said mockingly. 'What rubbish!' She continued.

'So, you don't believe in the curse?' he asked.

'Of course not. There is nothing unachievable, especially if you put your will into it. These old fanatics often spread rumours to support their agenda and yell about omens to all who would listen.'

'How can you be so sure of everything? What if he is right, and we will face the consequences?'

'Then we will figure it out together like we always do.' She assured, holding his hand tenderly.

Aryan grinned and trailed after her like an eager puppy. 'Oh Firdaus, God damn the day you came into my life. You're like that morsel of food stuck in my throat, something I can neither swallow nor spit.'

As they entered the hotel, Firdaus saw Sidharth sitting with a newspaper in his hand and eyes fixed on the door. 'What are you doing here?' She yelled.

'You think you can betray me, woman?' He folded his newspaper, got up and came close to her.

'Hey man, what's your problem? Don't talk to her like this.' Aryan interfered by pushing him back.

'You guys will not get away with this. Tell me, Sidharth said to Firdaus and Aryan, ' where is the Necklace?'

'We don't know.' Aryan replied almost instantly.

'Nonsense.' Sidharth said condescendingly.

'Don't take me for a fool, you two.' He admonished. 'Let me remind you, we had an agreement, and you're supposed to hold your part of the deal.' He announced. Sidharth thought he was overdoing his character for a second, but then his doubts cleared when Aryan chose his side and told Firdaus they were obligated to help him. 'Alright, I'll tell you where the Necklace is.' She spat out.

Aryan and Sidharth settled in Firdaus's room, awaiting her plan's revelation. She swung open the wooden doors of her cupboard and discreetly typed in a code to open the locker nestled between a shelf and a drawer. She pulled out her gun and dramatically loaded it with the bullets. 'What are you doing, Firdaus? Are you planning to carry a gun into the temple?' Aryan asked fretfully.

'Not just me. You both need guns, too. We will enter the temple with other worshipers through the main corridor to avoid attention. As the procession begins, we will sneak into the Sanctorum. Through the access shown by Mr Krishnamurthy, we will enter the underground tunnel leading us to the secret vaults.'

'How are we going to open the vault, Firdaus?' Sidharth asked with curiosity.

'As far as I know, they don't have any modern security system, so we will have to get the clue from the door's appearance. These old doors built for protection hardly open by applying labour. They often only open upon solving the riddle illustrated on the door.'

'What if we fail in solving the riddle?' Aryan asked nervously. 'We won't. I'll figure out a way to solve it.' She replied confidently.

'What a brilliant plan!' Sidharth remarked ironically. 'We don't know what awaits us down there, and all we are taking is a gun.'

'Yes, you're right; we don't know what is down there, and there is no way to know it until we go there personally.'

'So, we plan on shooting cockroaches and rats that dwell there?'

'Sure, if necessary, I'll shoot snakes and cockroaches.'

'What if there are invincible forces down there?' Asked Aryan.

'Ah!' Firdaus shuddered, 'then I don't know. They might, possess me and then I'll get to kill you without having to take the blame.' She joked. 'Everything is funny to you. Isn't it. Have you ever thought what would happen if the curse were for real?'

I don't bother myself with problems we haven't encountered yet, and I suggest you all should not bother as well. We will get through whatever awaits down there.'

'I am not convinced with your plan, but I don't have a choice, so I'll come along.' Sidharth sighed and declared.

'Alright then, we'll meet in the hotel lobby at dawn and march to the temple at 5 am.' The boys nodded in approval and went to their rooms to rest for the day.

Sidharth paced around the room, anxiously wondering why he hadn't received any word of communication from Maria. He opened his laptop and refreshed his email twice, eagerly waiting for his senior to provide further correspondence on what to do next. Sidharth never used his cell phone to discuss confidential matters. He was supplied with a burner phone or used hotel phones or telephone booths to communicate. He opened the door of his room to go to the lobby to make a phone call, but to his surprise, he saw Maria waiting outside his room, ready to knock. Maria glanced through the corridor, ensuring no one saw her, and then discreetly entered the room.

'I was waiting to hear from you, madam.' Sidharth said, locking his hands behind his back.

'You have done quite well till now, but I will personally handle this case moving forward.'

Sidharth dropped his head and asked, 'I understand I am crossing a line here, but I wish to know what you have decided? Aryan is a dear friend, and he is not at fault here. He was forced into this mission by the ASI, and if anything harms him, then I would like to know.'

'Don't worry, your friend is safe.' Maria assured.

'Unfortunately, I had to make some arrangements for Ms Durrani. She will not reach the temple tomorrow. That's all you need to know.' Sidharth exhaled a sigh of relief and began to pack.

Firdaus wandered around the flea market, searching for old books that could help her understand the history of the underground vaults. She was eager to know who built it and what inspired them to build something like that under the temple. She believed such information would help her solve the riddle.

While browsing the dusty books stacked in a small rustic shop at the very end of the flea market, she stumbled upon a book she used to read to her daughter. Rubbing off the dust from the cover, she saw a picture of the little girl standing next to the sheep. Ariana used to love the story of that little girl, Eva, who loved her sheep. Tears filled her eyes, and Firdaus walked out of the shop immediately. She took her burner phone out of her bag and called Debojeet.

She expected Debojeet to answer the phone, but her daughter responded instead. 'Hello,' she spoke in her innocent childish voice. 'Aru, my dearest.' Firdaus replied, choked with emotions.

'Mumma, where are you? I miss you.' The little one replied. Before Firdaus could say more, a gang of men attacked her. One hit her on the head, making her lose consciousness, and the others picked her up and shoved her into the black van.

As the evening progressed, Firdaus's disappearance worried Aryan. He had visited her room several times, but no one had answered the door. He tried calling her on her phone, which led straight to the voicemail. Assuming Sidharth would know of her whereabouts, he marched to his room and banged on the door with rage. Sidharth answered the door and invited him in.

'Mihir Agnihotri, where is Firdaus?' He frowned. Sidharth, a.k.a Mihir, said, 'I don't know, but my department has taken her somewhere. She will trouble us no more.'

'What have you done, Mihir?' Aryan roared.

'What have I done? I have done nothing but stop your friend from helping a terrorist.' Aryan winced upon hearing his words. 'What do you mean by that?

'Firdaus is working for Karim Khan, the international terrorist we have been looking for. He has funded this mission, and he is the one who seeks this necklace. He wants to trade this necklace in exchange for grenades, missiles, guns and what not.

'I don't believe you. Firdaus cannot do this.' 'Yes, she can do many things, but definitely not this.' Aryan defended her.

'It doesn't matter, Aryan. It's over. We have her, and my men are handling her as we speak.'

'What do you mean by handling her?' Ayan lunged out of the chair he was sitting on. Mihir chose silence over words at that instance and kept his gaze away from him. 'Answer me, Mihir, is she in danger?' Rage burning in his eyes. 'I don't know about that.' He said defensively. 'You know how things work. We're only given information that concerns us, and we're not allowed to ask more.'

'Listen to me, Mihir, if something happens to her, I will hunt you down and make you pay for it.' Aryan warned. 'Now tell me, where is she?' He asked with an unrelenting stare.

'Aryan, you know I can't do that. It's against my order.'

'You think I care.' Aryan held Mihir by the collar of his shirt. 'Tell me where she is?'

'Or what?'

He raised his hand to blow a punch on his face. 'Sure, go ahead, Aryan, hit me.'

Aryan took his hand off his collar, still enraged though. 'Please, Mihir, please, I beg you, tell me where she is, and I promise I'll convince her not to steal the necklace.' 'I'll personally report her to the authorities and ensure legal action is taken if she is found guilty.' He said shakily.

Mihir stared at him for a bit, trying to understand the depth of his friend's distress. 'You love her, don't you? 'Mihir, she is important to me, and I can't let anything happen to her.' He replied.

Unable to say no to his friend anymore, Mihir said, 'I am not sure, but I would try searching for her on one of the boats parked at the lagoon outside the city.

'Can you be more precise?' He insisted.

'I have told you everything I knew. Now make haste if you wish to save your friend.' Aryan motioned towards the door, and as he opened it, a concerning voice from behind echoed, 'don't do this, Aryan. Save yourself and get out of this mess.' He heard the warning and then shut the door behind him without responding.

* * *

Firdaus kneeled defenceless with hands raised in the air, surrendering herself to the group of men standing with guns against her. A white scarf was tied around her eyes, stained from the blood that dripped from her temples. 'What do you want?' Firdaus yelled. No response followed. After a few seconds, she cried again, 'please tell me what you want and why have you kidnapped me? This time, a response came through, 'You know why you're here.' The hollow voice seemed familiar.

'Have we met before?' She shuddered.

'My identity is of no relevance here. Maria said sharply. 'You'll only be told things you must know, and for now, all you need to know is you're not kidnapped but are in official custody and are obliged to comply with all our orders.'

'Oh, I had no idea. One was entitled under official capacity to kidnap someone at gunpoint.' Firdaus scoffed.

'Ms Durrani, you're bright and ambitious, and under normal circumstances, I would have appreciated your earnestness. However, this necklace you're after is exceptional, and although I commend your fervour, I can't let you have it. It is not yours to have.'

'Ma'am, I have been given the authority to find the necklace by the ASI.' Firdaus replied.

'I understand, but I have the authority to overrule ASI, and I have done that. This hunt is not official and, above all, not legal. Therefore, I suggest you let it go.' Maria retorted. 'Who are you, please tell me.' She pleaded. 'You don't need to know who I am, but I can tell you who I work for. R&AW.'

'Firdaus bit her lip angrily and exhaled in exasperation. 'It seems you're tired; believe me, we are too. We can end this if you tell me what you know about Karim Khan.'

'Karim Khan,' Firdaus repeated the name.

'I don't know any Karim Khan.' She replied.

'Well, if you don't know him, then why are you working for him?'

'I am not working for anyone.' She said firmly. 'Please let me go now.'

A moment of silence came through their conversation. 'I know you're doing this to save your daughter. Isn't that right, Ms?' Maria asked in a slightly sympathetic tone. Tears ran down her cheeks, drenching the scarf that blindfolded her. She rested her arms and dropped her shoulder in defeat. 'I'll tell you everything on one condition, and that is you first bring me food.' She snorted. Her demand surprised Maria for a second, but looking at her frail body and weekend spirit, her wish for food seemed just. A sense of pity filled her heart, and Maria agreed to arrange for dinner. She ordered her men to keep an eye on the woman while she got off the boat to get food.

Aryan furtively looked through dozens of houseboats parked next to each other before reaching the last one. He could see Firdaus tied to a chair, too frail and weak to even move. Spotting the armed men keeping an eye on Firdaus, Aryan motioned backwards to hide behind the palm trees. 'How am I going to fight them without my gun?' Aryan murmured out of distress. To distract them, he picked up a bunch of tweaks lying under the tree and threw them one by one on his opposite side. One of the men heard the sound and walked in the direction away from the boat to look for the cause of the sound. Taking the opportunity, Aryan slid from his hiding place towards the back of the boat, from where a window led him into the bedroom. Leaning to the wooden wall, Aryan motioned towards the corridor that connected the bedroom to the main deck. He swiftly moved his feet, walking on his toes to avoid the squeaky sound that might attract attention. He grabbed one of the men from behind, placing his hand on his waist and the other on his mouth and dragged him inside the room. The man punched him in the gut with his elbow to yank himself free from Aryan's grip.

As Aryan recoiled in pain, he pointed his gun at him and threatened to shoot. 'Don't move, or I'll shoot.' He warned. But Aryan didn't bother. He grabbed a lamp on the table beside him and lunged forward to hit him. He smacked the light on his head, making the man hit the ground with a terrific thud. Aryan took the gun from his immobile hand and lurched to the deck. The other three men fired gunshots at Aryan as he moved closer, but before the bullet could hit him, he ducked under the bar table and fired back from there, using the stone top as his shield. Firdaus squealed on hearing the gunshots and shook her head frenziedly to get rid of the blindfold. The sudden movement of her head allowed the scarf to loosen and slide down.

While the men were distracted by the intruder, Firdaus took the opportunity and dragged herself to the boat's edge, where she found the anchor, she used to cut the rope that tied her hands. She was too weak to fight, but to save Aryan, she hit one of the men with the chair, making him fall to the ground. Firdaus took his gun and fired a shot at the man in the corner who was focused on shooting Aryan. As he fell, Aryan caught the last guy and shot him in the leg.

Aryan strode towards Firdaus, who was about to faint, holding her while she dropped to the floor on her knees. 'Hey,' he gently patted her cheeks, 'don't give up now.' Aryan crooned. His voice was soft and soothing. Her eyelids dropped as she breathed slowly. 'Firdaus, please get up. We need to go.' He cried.

'I can't move. I am tired.' She whispered, resting her head on his shoulder, so Aryan picked her up in his arms and got off the boat.

He carried Firdaus to a houseboat parked next to the one they were in to stay put for a while. Aryan laid Firdaus on the bed and ran to the kitchen to fetch water. The kitchen was surprisingly luxurious and equipped with a coffee machine, a refrigerator filled with milk bottles, water bottles and some fresh vegetables, a toaster, and a pantry with packets of sugar, salt, pepper, rice crackers and chips. Aryan grabbed two bottles of water from the fridge and an apple and a banana from the fruit basket on the kitchen island and walked back to the room. He sprinkled a few drops of water on Firdaus's face to bring her to consciousness. As the icy cold droplets hit her cheeks, she gradually opened her eyes, coming back to life. 'Here, eat this.' Aryan offered a banana while biting his apple. She peeled the banana and took a bite that felt like a piece of heaven to her. She was so hungry that she took big bites and finished eating the banana in seconds.

'Is there more food?' She asked.

'Yes, there are packets of rice crackers and potato chips in the pantry.' He replied. She grabbed the packet of rice crackers from the pantry, ripped it open and shoved a handful of salty crisps in her mouth.

'Do you want coffee?' Asked Aryan.

'Yes, please.' She replied, crunching on crackers.

'Firdaus, why is everyone trying to kill you?' He asked, pouring the milk into two mugs.

'Well, because I have infuriated many people, including you, thank god you're not running after me with a knife in your hand.' She smirked.

Aryan grinned and replied, 'I think I am immune now.'

The injured men had called for help, and Maria and her team had arrived at the location. Aryan could see a few people getting off the ambulance and carrying the injured men into the vehicle. After a few minutes, two police cars arrived, and four officers, including Mihir, joined Maria and her group.

'Firdaus, I think these guys will soon come looking for us.'

'If we get out of this boat now, we will be caught.' She said fearfully. 'We should hide in the closet until they're gone.' He suggested.

'I agree. Let us go.' She threw the packet of crackers in the water and sneaked into the closet. Aryan spilled the milk in the drain and cleaned the mugs before putting them back onto the shelf. After making sure the kitchen looked unused, he went to the bedroom and got into the closet with Firdaus.

'I think this is a stupid plan.' She whispered.

'Do you have a better idea?' He asked in a hushed tone. 'No,' she answered sheepishly. 'Well then, here we are.' Soon, they heard footsteps coming toward the bedroom. Firdaus placed her hand on her mouth and held her breath for a few seconds to avoid making any noise. She anxiously held Aryan's hand and squeezed it tight. As her sweaty palms clenched against his hand, Aryan thought getting into the closet with Firdaus was indeed a bad idea.

She started sweating profusely and breathed erratically. She was out of breath and claustrophobic. Aryan saw the blood wear out of her face, making her look sick and pale. He had to do something, act fast to save her from fainting. He pulled her close and gently kissed her lips, taking her by surprise. She froze and blinked twice to comprehend what had just happened, but before she could make any sense of it, he kissed her again, locking his lips against hers and placing his hands on her cheeks. Now that he had her so close, her breath speeded with a desire to kiss him back. Her eyes glazed with passion, and she thought in that exact second that if she did not kiss him, she'd explode. When her lips covered his, and her tongue wiggled in his mouth, his heartbeat pulsated through the chest, making every inch of his body burn in desire.

'Did you find her?' Maria asked the men.

'No, ma'am. We don't think she is here,' one of the men replied.

'Then, why are you wasting your time?' She snapped. 'Check other boats, nearby shops, hotels, every place she could have gone. I want you all to find her before sunrise.' Her stern voice echoed. As the footsteps retrieved, Firdaus jerked back and pushed open the closet door.

'I am sorry, I was trying to calm you down.' Said Aryan. She scowled at him and then flounced out of the room. 'Firdaus, stop, I said; I am sorry.' Aryan ran after her. She drank half a bottle of water to calm down and then stomped the bottle on the table.

'Firdaus, they're still here. Please calm down, or they'll catch us.' She glared at him as her cheeks flushed. 'I am sorry.' Aryan repeated shamefully.

'No, Aryan, I am sorry; I am sorry for everything I have put you through. You don't deserve any of this.' She said with tears in her eyes.

'It doesn't matter what I deserve because I know you won't be able to give me that.' He paused for a second and then continued, 'all I wanted from you was the truth, but you always lied.' He said with disappointment in his voice.

'I don't want to lie anymore, Aryan, but I can't tell you the truth either. All I can say is that my life depends on this necklace.'

'Why can't you tell me the truth? Why is it so difficult? He grunted. 'It's not as easy as you think.' She snapped.

'Who is Karim Khan, and why are you working for him?'

'I don't know this man. I can swear on my life.' She had an earnest expression on her face.

'I am really tired, Firdaus. I don't know who I should believe anymore.'

'What do you mean?'

'Sidharth is not who he says he is, he is Mihir, ex CBI, current R&AW officer and my friend.'

'Oh, so you knew who he was, and you lied to me?' Firdaus snapped.

'You shouldn't be angry at someone lying to you when all you have done is lie and be deceitful.'

Firdaus, now frustrated with Aryan's unending list of accusations, said, 'Then why did you come to save me?'

'If my presence is tormenting every inch of your soul, then why don't you leave?'

'Because I love you,' he said, pausing to let his words sink into her mind. 'Even though your lies and betrayals have killed me from within, I still choose to love you. It's true, you're a bane of my existence, and yet here I am at your mercy, declaring my love only to be betrayed again.'

'That is not true.' She uttered vehemently. 'I have never betrayed you, Aryan. Yes, I lied, probably broke your heart but never betrayed you. That night five years ago, I stole the jewellery and sold it to a black-market dealer. The burden of this act grew with each passing day, and there came the point where my regret overpowered my sensibility. So, I stole the jewels once again and gave them to Dhimant. When I met him, I got to know you had not mentioned to him anything about our discovery and probably since you still believe I betrayed you, I assume he never told you the jewels were returned to him.'

'How do I know you're telling me the truth? 'He asked doubtfully.

'Do you remember the men who attacked us in Rajasthan? They worked for the black-market dealer who paid me to steal the jewellery. Because I stole it back from him, he has been looking for me ever since. In five years, I have changed many accommodations, cities and even my jobs to hide from him. It hasn't been easy, but I have done it because I love you too.' She quickly regretted confessing her feelings.

'I want to believe you.' Aryan uttered with tears in his eyes.

'Then please believe me.' She brought herself close to him and held his hand.

'Promise me, you'll never betray me again.'

'I promise I won't do anything to hurt you ever again.'

She leaned forward and kissed him. Aryan couldn't resist and kissed her back. His heart swelled with affection as he held her close. It felt as though every fibre of his being resisted her influence, yet his mind was consumed and powerless. Aryan was always aware that he was betraying his ethics and the values he stood for at every turn, yet he yielded to Firdaus's every whim and desire. 'Let's get this necklace and save your life from whoever or whatever you fear.' He declared. Firdaus smiled and smothered him with kisses all over his face. 'I love you so much.' She confessed.

Chapter 9

Padmanabhaswamy Temple, Thiruvananthapuram

The thin arc appeared at the horizon as the sun began to rise, and the soft rays reflected the temple's arches, gilding them with light. Travellers had stopped at the pond nestled in front of the temple to witness the natural formation of a stunning silhouette of the temple in the still water. The temple guardians had taken up cleaning and organising chores and the local worshipers had joined them in preparations for the parade. The corridor was swept clean, and a majestic red carpet was spread across from the gopuram to the temple entrance to embellish the procession area. At 6 am, the sanctum doors were opened by Anand Krishnamurthy, the leading guardian of the temple. He was dressed in a silk off-white dhoti (a sarong) appropriate for the puja and marched through the sanctum chanting the peace mantra, ceremoniously spritzing Gangajal (holy water of river Ganges) on the deity of Lord Vishnu.

Firdaus got up with a spinning head, burning chest and throbbing temples. Her forehead was bruised, and her body was sore from last night's scuffle. She had gotten up later than she was supposed to and had no time to gather her thoughts as the procession was about to begin. She quickly lunged out of bed and walked towards the deck to look for Aryan. Aryan had gotten up before her and had gone to the market to pick up clothes.

He hopped on the boat handing her a bag of clothes, 'here, I have got you a saree. Please get ready as soon as you can.' Firdaus looked confused as she took the bag from his hand. 'What's wrong with my clothes?' She asked. 'If you intend to reach the sanctum without being noticed, you'll have to wear what everyone else is wearing. These clothes will help us to blend in.' He said, sliding into his sarong.

They entered the temple with everyone else through the gopuram and stood on the side where the crowd had gathered to get a glimpse of the mighty deity of their God. The guardians carried the supine deity of Lord Vishnu out of the sanctum, chanting sacred mantras that echoed through the temple.

'So, what's the plan now?' Aryan whispered in her ears.

'When the procession begins, we will slowly move through the crowd to reach the sanctum, and from there, we will find the way to the vaults.' She replied.

'I hope it's as easy as you make it sound,' he muttered.

The mantra chanting grew louder as the crowd joined, bowing their heads in front of the deity being paraded. Firdaus made her way through the overwhelming crowd. When she reached the stairs that led to the sanctum, she stopped and turned back to make sure Aryan was following. While she had managed to sneak into the temple without calling for the security guard's attention, she saw that Aryan was caught trying to sneak in and was led back to the crowd. She hid behind the door to wait for Aryan, signalling him to enter the temple through the back door of the administrator's office.

Aryan moved through the crowd in the opposite direction and reached the office. It was locked, so Aryan picked up a stone lying next to the door and broke the lock to get in. The cracking of the lock would have been audible, but the cheering crowd and the loud chanting of mantras made it easy for him to break in without being noticed.

In the meantime, Firdaus slid the heavy concrete slab surfaced beneath the statue and looked through the stairs that blended into the darkness. She glanced through the sanctum and strode straight to the Havan-Kund, a brass basket full of wooden logs. She tore a piece of cloth from her saree, tied it around the top of the wood log and then dipped it into the bowl of oil to light fire. 'How the hell did you get here without being noticed.' Asked Aryan blithely, entering the temple from the back door. He saw Firdaus standing with a burning log.

'What are you doing?' He shouted.

'I found the way to the vaults.' She replied, pointing at the stairs that sheathed the vaults.

'I'll lead the way.' She said, climbing down the stairs.

'Of course,' Aryan murmured, following her.

'This looks like a crypt.'

'Firdaus, I hate to admit it, but I am scared.' His voice shredded by fear. '

'Common Aryan, there is nothing to be scared off, at least not yet.' She murmured the last part under her breath.

'You know I am scared of snakes and scorpions; generally, all crypts and dungeons are filled with those dreadful creatures. I have seen it in movies.'

'Aryan stop thinking about it and Just keep walking.'

Firdaus lost her balance momentarily walking on the damp and slippery floor. Hence, she held the structure on her right to save herself from falling on her head. That metal structure felt like a statue under her hand, and as she turned the torch around, she found that she was holding onto the figure of the Hindu God, Ganesh. She moved the log to the perpendicular position to see what lay ahead of the statue. She was stunned to find there were other statues of different gods and demigods placed at an equal distance next to each either, forming a row. 'Aryan, look!' She said excitedly. 'Oh my god!' He exclaimed.

The treasure vaults on the left were guarded by thick floor-to-ceiling iron doors. Every vault was assigned an alphabet etched on the top of the door. 'Firdaus, we're never going to find the necklace. There are four vaults. This necklace could be in any one of them.'

Firdaus moved closer to vault B and threw the light on the door. 'My guess is that the necklace is inside vault B.'

'How sure are you?'

Don't know. It's a gut feeling, kinda like an instinct.'

'Then let's go in there.' Firdaus turned to Aryan and looked at him nervously.

'We should trust your instincts.' He smiled.

'What if the necklace is not in here.' She asked shakily.

'Then we look for it in the other vault.' Aryan paused for a second and then continued, 'Your instincts in such matters exceed any logical explanation and I have learnt to trust them. You should, too.'

Firdaus brought the burning log closer to the door to see what was engraved and etched on the wall-like iron door. And the frame, as thick as a tree trunk, was covered by the carvings of other reptiles spiralling through the top, where a ferocious demon head looked down on the door with his tongue out as if he'd eat anyone who entered the vault without his permission. It was debatable if that ferocious head belonged to a demon or a demigod. Still, it was clear that the predator was there to guard the snakes and protect the door.

As she moved closer, she noticed a text box between the engraved cobras where something was written in Sanskrit. 'The one who removes my poison befriends me, and the one who destroys my poison becomes my master.' She read out loud.

'What does this mean?' Aryan wiped the drops of sweat that had formed on his forehead.

'Well, this is a riddle. I was expecting something like this.' She replied.

'How are we going to solve this?'

Firdaus's eyes moved too quickly from one direction to another. 'Do you have a phone?' She asked, standing befuddled.

'I do, but the battery is dead.'

'Well, then we'll have to rely on our memory and instincts.'

'What do you mean?' Aryan asked nervously. Firdaus did not respond and lunged to the other side of the corridor, where statues of various gods were placed in a line.

'This is Ganpati Ji,' she said, pointing at the statue, 'this is one of Vishnu's avatars. This is Brahma, and this is,' she took a pause. 'Garuda, the demigod.' Aryan cut in. Firdaus turned around dramatically and asked, 'do you remember the mantra they chanted when they began the parade?'

'Yes, it was the Garuda mantra. My mother would chant it 108 times before my examinations. I don't think it mostly worked, but it gave her peace of mind.'

Her expression suddenly changed, and her face lit up with excitement. 'I think I know how to open the door!'

'As per the Garuda Upanishad (an old Hindu scripture), Garuda the demigod had a bird's face and a human's body. The mount of Lord Vishnu and eternal foe of serpents, this eagle-man had the power to destroy the venom.'

'And according to the text mentioned on the door, if we destroy the venom from the cobras, we can master them, meaning they won't harm us and would let us enter the vault.' Aryan added.

'Yes, and if my theory is right, then this (Eagle-man) Garuda statue hoards the door's key.'

She carefully picked up the statue from its stand and kept aside. Aryan checked the stand to see if it had a secret place where a key could have been hidden but found nothing. Firdaus jerked the statue, thinking the key would drop out of it any minute.

Unfortunately, to her dismay, she found nothing coming forth. 'Did we get this wrong?' Aryan asked anxiously. 'The key has to be somewhere here.' She said assertively.

'Now I have my doubts.' He shrugged.

Firdaus stared at the statue for a few seconds. 'Wait a minute. The deity is missing its beak.' She realized. 'What beak?' Aryan asked in astonishment.

'This half-eagle and half-human god is supposed to have a beak. In the Upanishad (the holy scripture), it is mentioned that Garuda had round eyes, golden wings and a kite's beak.'

They exchanged a look and then hurried to find the beak. Aryan searched for the wavy-edged narrow beak around the stand by moving his finger across the structure.

'Did you find anything?' Firdaus yelled from a distance.

'No, not yet. I need the light.'

'Wait, I am coming.' She strode to Aryan and gave him the burning log.

He swung the log and threw light on the door on the opposite side. 'Let's check for a clue on the door.' 'You're getting smarter every day, Aryan. She smiled. The door carvings were intricate and mostly covered in spider webs. Aryan moved his hands through the spiralling snake design, making a ghastly face and stumbled upon a small hole entangled by the tail of one of the cobras. He inserted his finger inside the hole until he touched something that hurt his finger. His cheeks turned pink as he tried to pull the pointy substance out of the hole. 'I think I found it.' He said with a grin.

Firdaus attached the beak to the statue and placed it back on the stand. Within seconds, a small piece of marble pulled out of the stand on its own, giving access to the key behind it. Firdaus's eyes filled with tears as she scooped up the key. 'Is this what I think it is?' She asked, biting her lower lip. 'Yes... Yes, Firdaus. It is. Now get your bloody necklace so we can go home.' He yelled in excitement.

As she took the key out of the stand, they immediately heard the clicking sound of the shutters covering the vent, creating a complete vacuum inside the corridor in a matter of seconds. Before they could react, the shutter uncovered the vent and forced out poisonous gas through the space, making them both cough profusely.

'What the hell just happened.' She said in between her coughs. 'I thought we found the key.' 'I don't think this is the right key.' Firdaus covered her mouth with the loose end of her saree. 'If we don't find the right key, we'll die soon.' Aryan feared. 'Don't state the obvious. Just do something.' She retorted. 'This key should have some significance if it unleashed the poisonous gas. He staggered his way to the door and read out the riddle again. 'The one who removes my poison befriends me,' his voice echoed. Perhaps this key signifies that the poison these snakes endured once is now in our lungs, which makes us one of them.' He said with a doubtful expression.

Firdaus dropped to the ground, trying to grasp a breath.

'Are you okay?' Aryan caught her by her hand.

'I am fine.'

'Firdaus, just wait a little longer. I'll figure a way out for us.' He promised. 'What was the last part of the riddle?' She asked, holding her head. 'One who destroys my poison becomes my master.' Aryan reread the text.

'We have to find something that destroys the poison.' She stated in a faint murmur.

'Firdaus... Firdaus, wake up.' Aryan cried. 'You knew about the demigod Garuda, which means you have read the Upanishad. The answer to this riddle would surely be in that text. Firdaus, are you listening?' He gently patted her cheeks to get her to consciousness.

'How are you still breathing?'

'I was a state-level swimmer. I know how to hold my breath. Now, please try to focus. We don't have time. Who or what helped Garuda to destroy the poison?

'I don't remember. I read it a while ago.' She murmured.

'Firdaus, if you don't try, we'll die here.'

'I need wa… ter.'

'Hold your breath. It'll help you.' He lunged into his bag and took out a bottle of water.

'It was a thunderbolt. God Indra's thunderbolt aided in the killing of the venom.' She said, gulping down the water.

'Are you sure?'

'I am positive.'

Aryan moved forward to the marble stand on which the deity of Garuda was laid and began to push it. The stand was heavy, and Aryan could only move it half an inch, holding his breath, so he pushed it multiple times, but the stand hardly moved. With all his strength, he tried one final time, and the stand plunged to the ground, breaking into pieces that scattered all over the place.

The metal locker emerged from the ground as the stand got out of the way. Aryan inserted the key into the lock and turned it around to unlock the safe. The thunderbolt identical to Indra's weapon, also called Vajra in Sanskrit lay under it. The lotus bud-shaped, four-pronged Vajra was believed to hoard extraordinary powers used for the destruction of evil. Aryan pulled the brass weapon out of the locker and placed it between the cobras. As he solved the last piece of the riddle, the door opened, and oxygen flowed through the vents again.

* * *

Tons of gold in the form of bricks lay behind the door. As they walked past it, they spotted dozens of statues and artifacts made from rare materials kept in a cluster on the side of the room. From chests filled with all kinds of jewels to precious silverware and platinum furniture, vault B had treasure one could have never imagined.

'I don't have words to describe how I feel right now.' Aryan exclaimed.

'If we could take all these, we would become rich.' She suggested trying to catch her breath.

'And end up in jail. No, thank you.'

'Why can't you behave like a normal person for once.' She grunted, whisking her way through the treasure.

'And you think you're normal?'

'Give me a break. Will you?'

'Fine, let's just take what we have come for and leave. And promise me you won't touch anything else. You don't want to steal from a temple. That brings curse.'

'Oh my god. Is he serious?' She muttered in frustration.

A small wooden chest was kept behind the golden statues of Lord Krishna and his beloved Radha, which somehow attracted Firdaus's attention. She opened it and found the Patiala necklace rolled into a semi-circle to fit in the box. The centre diamond glowed brightly, making Firdaus lose her sight for a second.

'This is breathtaking.' She said, holding the necklace close to her neck.

'I can't believe we found it.' Aryan cried out of happiness.

Holding the necklace gave her the confidence that now she would be able to save her daughter. She was so close to telling Aryan how happy she felt at that moment, but she withheld her emotions, thinking telling the truth would only devastate him.

Their moment of victory was, however, short-lived. Maria and her team of agents marched into the vault, dropping smoke bombs on their way, filling up the space with smoke as they exploded. The smoke in the vault made breathing difficult for Aryan and Firdaus. They dropped to the ground with heavy chests. The necklace slipped out of her grip as she lay flat on the surface, taking short breaths through her mouth. The smoke blocked his sight, so Aryan dragged his body towards her, stretching his arm to hold hers. 'Firdaus…' He cried loudly.

She stretched her arm forward to reach for his hand, but before reaching him, a tall man with a broad-built caught Aryan and took him away. Although her vision was blocked by the smoke, she could see the blurry silhouette of that tall man standing over Aryan, putting the oxygen mask on his face. She slightly tilted her head to get a better vision of him, and as her eyes moved up to his face, she froze at the sight of the man talking to Maria. 'Sidharth.' She whispered fretfully.

As he motioned towards Firdaus, Maria stopped him and said, 'I got her, don't worry.' She took the other mask from his hand and placed it on her nose. She lifted her head to tighten the grip and then called for a stretcher to take her to the hospital.

'Mother, is that you?' A faint voice came through the oxygen mask.

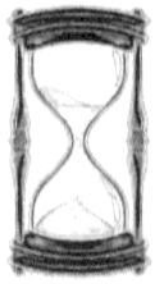

Chapter 10
Mumbai

'Let me go.' Firdaus shouted in retaliation as the door flew open and Maria entered. She tried to pull her wrist out of the handcuff. 'I said let me go.' She repeated authoritatively.

Maria turned on the tube light above her head, making Firdaus squint to defend herself from the harsh light going straight into her eyes. 'Turn off this stupid light. It's hurting my eyes.' She yelled.

Neither overly attractive nor typically average looking, the fifty-two-year-old R&AW agent had an erudite appeal - wisps of grey strands in her dark brown hair, big eyes and an arrestingly deep voice that could make a room fall silent. Maria cleaned her thick-rim glasses and placed them back above her forehead. 'Don't waste your breath, Firdaus.' She replied grimly.

'Where am I?'

'You were not happy with our treatment last time, so we brought you to a proper interrogation room this time.' She replied. Firdaus snorted loudly in exasperation. 'Where is Aryan?' She asked. Maria ignored her question and sat primly on the opposite side of the desk, smoothing out the creases of her skirt. She kept the notepad on the table and clicked her pen to take notes.

'Tell me, how do you know Karim Khan?' She asked.

'I don't know him. How many times am I supposed to tell you that?'

'Don't make this harder, Firdaus.' She glared at her. Firdaus glared back, incensed. 'Unless you don't change your question, my answer will be the same. 'I don't know anyone called Karim Khan.'

The woman's expression hardened, and her voice turned sharp. 'Alright then, tell me who kidnapped your daughter?' Firdaus restrained from answering that question. 'Look, you'll have to answer my questions eventually. The longer you'll take, the more difficult it'll be for us to save your daughter.' Her tone mellowed.

'As if you care, mother.' She snapped. Maria flinched upon getting called mother.

Heralding the persona of a disciplinarian, Maria was an objectively driven, fierce, and a headstrong woman. She had earned the moniker 'The affable dictator' through her legendary manipulative skills, capable of reducing anyone to submission. Her mastery of literature, art, and human psychology elevated her to the status of one of the most intelligent women in her fraternity. It was widely believed that she could hardly make a mistake, let alone a blunder this huge. The unspoken whispers among her colleagues sent chills down her spine. How had she failed to anticipate this moment?

Mihir looked at his colleague in surprise. 'Mother?' He whispered. His other colleague kept staring at Maria and Firdaus through the glass window. 'She knew all this time and she didn't bother to tell us.' He seemed like the person who would report everything that happened in the field to the big man sitting in the office.

Maria cleared her throat and said, 'I do care for every innocent life that's in danger. And because of you, your daughter's life is at stake.'

'Oh, don't worry. I know very well how to take care of my child.'

'Firdaus, I care for the child whose life is in danger. Please try to cooperate, we're only trying to help you.'

'Why am I surprised to know that you care for everyone but me.' She scoffed.

'I know you're angry and have all the right to be angry with me, but this case is bigger than you and I. You have to save your daughter, and we must catch a terrorist preparing to kill millions of innocent people as we speak.'

She leaned forward and held her hand. 'I want to help you, Firdaus. Please let me help you.' She whispered in a soft tone. Firdaus pulled the hand from beneath hers, giving her a scornful expression.

'He came to the library every day for the past six months. We didn't speak much for the first couple of months, but then he asked for my suggestions on books. I thought he wanted to impress the nerdy librarian with his polished mannerisms, manly charm, and thirst for knowledge. Yet it turns out he wanted more than just my attention.'

'And when did he meet your daughter?'

'We started dating. So, he would come home to spend time with me and that's when he got close to Ariana.'

'So, you and Karim were dating.' She scribbled something on her notepad.

'Debojeet Bagchi, that's how he addressed himself.'

'Mr Bagchi? The businessman from Calcutta?'

'Yes. He is the one who abducted my daughter.'

'How is he involved in all this?'

'Isn't that your job to find out?'

Maria ignored her jibe and continued, 'has he ever mentioned Karim Khan in his conversation with you?'

'Oh my god, I had no idea you sucked at your job.' She leaned forward and asked, 'did you abandon me for this?' Maria's face turned pale as she lunged out of the chair. It was harder to face her daughter than she thought initially.

'I have to take a break.' She muttered nervously.

'Go ahead, Mother, shun me once again.'

Mihir was listening to their conversation from behind the glass window that looked like a mirror from the room where Firdaus was being interrogated. Upon hearing Mr Bagchi's name, he thought of Aryan, who had called him to get information on a licensed gun that belonged to him. For a few minutes, he collected his thoughts and tried to connect the dots between

Karim and Debojeet. As a possible explanation struck his brain, his eyes twinkled, and he rushed into the interrogation room.

'Maria, I need to speak to you.'

'Not now, Mihir.'

'Ma'am, this is urgent.'

'I thought you were a royal?' Firdaus turned her head to Mihir. He did not respond to her. 'I'll be out in a minute.' Said Maria. 'Thank you.' He dropped his chin in acknowledgement.

Firdaus glared at her mother in disgust as she left the room to speak to her colleague.

'We have to track Bagchi's movements.' Mihir explained.

'You think he is involved.'

'Yes, he is. Firdaus is telling the truth.'

'How do you know?'

'So, a few days ago…..' he narrated the incident and concluded by saying 'that gun belonged to Bagchi.'

'This means she is telling the truth, and we have got this wrong.' Maria said with fear in her voice.

Mihir nodded and said, 'Maybe Karim is not involved.'

'But our intel can't be wrong.' Maria sighed; her tone tinged with perplexity.

'There is only one possibility then: Bagchi is working with Khan.' I think you're right.

Maria thought of a plan that could lead them to Khan, and she rushed back to the interrogation room to tell Firdaus that she had found a way to save her daughter.

Firdaus was peering at the mirror when Maria walked in again.

'How many people are watching us right now?' She asked, moving her eyes to the mirror.

'Does it matter?' She didn't respond.

'Firdaus, I have got a plan to save your daughter.'

Firdaus looked curious. 'You must give the necklace to Mr Bagchi.' Said Maria. Firdaus's eyes widened with shock. 'What?' 'Yes, we're going to give him the necklace, but not the one you think.'

'Oh no, no, no-no. You can't fool him with the fake necklace.' Firdaus jumped out of her chair. 'It is my daughter's life at stake here. I am not taking any chances.'

'Don't worry, before he realises that he has the replica, we'll catch him and through him Karim Khan.' She said with confidence.

'And what if he gets to know before you catch him? You really think he'll give me my Ariana without making sure the necklace is authentic?' She rolled her eyes.

'We won't give him that time.' 'Didn't he ask you to get the necklace in ten days?

Yes, Firdaus answered.

'This means he is bound by time.'

'He said he wants the necklace found in ten days.' Said Firdaus. 'Great! And today is the eighth day, isn't it?' Maria asked. Firdaus nodded.

'We get the replica from Rajasthan by tomorrow, and you give it to him late at night so that he has no time to check its authenticity.'

'Are you sure this is going to work?' Firdaus asked, not wholly convinced. 'It should work.'

Maria said, unlocking the handcuffs, 'you can go home now, but please don't try to act smart. Just have faith in us.' She nodded, adjusting the pleats of her saree.

As she reached the door, a voice came from behind. 'Firdaus, I am sorry.' She turned around and saw her mother in tears.

'I just…' Maria tried to let out a sentence, but all she could manage after 'I just' was an exhaling sound of her breath. 'You should know I had to do what I did.' She finally spat out. Firdaus's unnerving gaze pierced her heart. 'I had to get out of that marriage and away from the life I had once chosen. Your father was a good man but religious and conservative. He had unknowingly strangled my dreams and ambitions. I had to break free to save myself. I am so sorry that I had to let you go, too. But my dear, sometimes in life, you don't have a choice.' She choked with regret.

'You always have a choice.' Firdaus announced dramatically, contradicting her. 'You chose to abandon me. You chose to save yourself at my cost, and it was your choice to be callous, mother. So, don't tell me you had no choice.'

Maria's eyes narrowed as she looked down. 'I hope you have it in your heart to forgive me one day.' Firdaus didn't respond and stormed out of the room slamming the door behind her.

* * *

'How dare you?' Aryan fumed. 'I am sorry.' Firdaus apologised. He brought his closed fist near his mouth and exhaled loudly. 'Aryan, please calm down.' She said in fear.

He wrenched his hand free, face flooded with anger, 'Five years, Firdaus. In these five years, you never mentioned that we have a daughter together?'

'I was afraid that you would take her away from me.' She broke down in tears. 'You despised me, Aryan. What else could I have thought?' She cried.

'Firdaus, you kept my daughter away from me for five years. I despise you even more now.' He let his head fall into his hands for a few moments before looking back up. When he spoke again, his voice became achingly sad. 'Where is she, Firdaus?' He asked.

'She is taken away from me for that bloody necklace.' Her eyes narrowed as she sank onto the couch.

'What do you mean?'

Firdaus leaned forward and held his hand. 'Aryan, our daughter, is kidnapped.' She said with watery eyes. 'For the necklace?' Firdaus nodded, getting up on her shaky feet. 'We're going to give them the replica we saw in Rajasthan in exchange for our daughter.'

Aryan regained his composure to attend to the matter at hand. He was mad at her for not telling him the truth earlier, but he knew there was no time for expressing his disappointment. 'You think this is going to work?' His voice instantly mellowed.

'I don't know, but this is our best option.'

'How are we going to get the replica?

'Let that be my mother's problem.' She continued, 'all I know is that I'll have the necklace by this evening, and I'll give it to Debojeet tonight.'

'Your mother? I thought she was dead.' He asked curiously.'

'I have to fill you in on a lot of updates. For now, all you need to know is that Maria Saldana is Mariam Durrani, my mother.'

Aryan looked confused. 'What do you mean? How is she alive? Why hasn't she made any effort to get in touch with you? What's going on?' There was an overwhelming amount of information to process, and his brain felt too shaky to comprehend anything.

'I'll tell you everything, but first I need to go and meet Debojeet Bagchi who has our daughter.'

'I'll come with you.'

'I don't think you should. Maria thinks I should keep you out of this.' She paused for a second and then said, 'for your safety.'

'What the hell are you talking about? I am the agent, and you're the civilian here. If someone should go, it is I and not you.' He raised one of his eyebrows in disbelief.

'Okay, fine, I don't want to argue. Come if you want.'

They left to go to Bagchi's apartment to meet him. His penthouse in Mumbai was monstrously massive and ghoulishly empty. The furniture was cloaked with white bed sheets, and the floor was covered in dust and cobwebs. As they entered through the door, which was surprisingly open, the cold wind coming from the open window rushed through their faces. 'Are we in the right apartment?' Aryan asked, making his way through the unattended newspapers and letters lying on the splintered floor.

'I was given this address. Look.' She showed him Bagchi's message on her phone. 'Something is wrong. Why is he not here?' Firdaus muttered.'

The apartment had no electricity. Firdaus maneuvered through it, holding onto the furniture as she moved and used her hands to know what lay ahead her. Aryan dove for Firdaus; 'watch out!' he screamed as she hit the lamp, stumbled, and ultimately slammed into the floor. He turned on his phone's flashlight and offered his hand to pick her up. 'Are you okay?'

'Yes, I'm fine.' She replied, rubbing off the dust from her pants.

I don't understand. This apartment looks unoccupied for years. Are you sure he gave you the right address? Aryan checked the message on her phone. 'He had to be here.' Firdaus said anxiously.

They heard the telephone ring in the distance and darted to the room from where the sound was coming. Firdaus scooped up the phone after the fourth ring and asked, 'Debojeet is that you?'

'I told you to come alone, and you came with an agent.' His menacing voice made her nervous.

'Where is my daughter?' Aryan interrupted.

'She is with me. And please spare me, don't hurt my daughter, or I'll kill your bravado.'

'We had a deal, Debojeet. I have the necklace you want.' Said Firdaus gesturing Aryan to remain silent.

'I know you have kept your part of the deal. Now you have to do one last thing for me.'

'What is it?' Aryan snapped.

'I want Firdaus to come to London with the necklace.'

'Why?'

'Mr Verma, I suggest you stay out of this.' Aryan was boiling with rage, 'what the...' but Firdaus did not let him speak further. She held his arm, signalling him to remain silent. 'I'll come wherever you want me to, just please don't hurt my daughter.' She pleaded.

'There is a plane ticket for you on the dining table. I'll see you at Heathrow tomorrow.' A disconnected tone came through the telephone as he hung up.

Chapter 11

London, United Kingdom

The black sedan that picked up Firdaus from the airport was now driving alongside Hyde Park, making its way to The National Gallery in Trafalgar Square. Firdaus had no idea where she was being taken, but she knew what she had to do no matter where she met Bagchi. She kept her communication limited with the driver and gazed out the window throughout the drive.

The car deposited the passenger outside the national gallery, and the driver informed her that she had to go meet 'the boss' in room number 01. She opened her backpack and grabbed the recording device from it. As she entered the gallery, she looked for the signboard that displayed directions for the toilets and followed the map. Firdaus pulled the third button from her shirt, unstitched it from the fabric and glued the white recorder that looked like a button in its place. She washed her face, combed her hair and assured herself she could do this.

Room number 01 had a magnificent display of paintings & sculptures from the European High Renaissance. She glanced across the room to find Bagchi and saw the middle-aged man sitting across Raphael's Resurrection of Christ on a marble bench. 'Welcome to London Firdaus.' He said, bringing his mouth close to her ear.

'I have the necklace you asked for.' Her voice was stern, and her face looked grim.

'Can we just enjoy seeing this beautiful painting for a while?' He said flippantly.

'You really think I would be interested in this when my daughter is in danger?' Her eyes flashed fire at him.

'Calm down, Firdaus. I assure you she is safe.'

'I want to be done with this. Just take your necklace and give me my daughter back.'

'Alright, I think you're not in the mood to appreciate art.'

'Of course, I am not.' She scoffed.

Debojeet bounced up from the bench and said, 'Let's go.'

'Where?' She asked.

'Mr Charles Brown will be here any minute now. We're going to sell the necklace to him. If the meeting goes well, I'll have my money, and you'll have your daughter.'

A petite man with an employee batch escorted them to room 55. Charles 's chestnut hair ruffled in the breeze as his head whipped back to look at Bagchi. He walked to the door to welcome his guest. 'I have chosen this venue for the International Art & Antiquity exhibition. How is it?' There was exhilaration in his voice.

'It is excellent. Well ventilated, cosy and right up your alley.' Bagchi replied with a smile.

Charles reached for Firdaus's hand and kissed it gently. 'Is this the talented young lady you were talking about?' 'Yes, she is the one.' He said, holding her other hand.

'May I ask the meaning of your name?'

'It means heaven.' She replied, her face stiff as marble.

'Your name is as beautiful as you are, Ms.'

'Where are my mannerisms? I held you two for too long at the door. You must come in, please.' He led the way.

'For God's sake, leave my hand, or I'll punch you in the face.' She hissed. Bagchi let go of her hand and whispered, 'sorry.' His face still expressed frivolousness.

'So, where is the necklace? I am so excited to see it.' Charles rubbed his hand out of excitement. Firdaus pulled out a velvet box from her backpack and kept it on the table. The necklace sparkled in the sunlight that beamed through the window.

'I can't believe you found it.' He said with a twinkle in his eye.

'I told you, I'll personally bring your treasure to London.'

'I know, and I am very grateful to you for keeping your part of the deal.'

Charles offered a friendly handshake.

'It's your turn now.'

'I know.' He admitted. He opened his bag and pulled out an envelope. 'Half cash and half bank transfer. Will that work for you?' He asked. Bagchi nodded. 'Great. So, our deal is done.' Charles said with a grin.

'There is one more thing I want from you.'

'Yes, go ahead and ask for anything.'

'Karim Khan needs to stay away from London until I reach India.'

'Done. I'll let the aviation operations know.' He paused for a few seconds and then said, 'I thought Mr Khan and you were friends.' Firdaus moved her gaze to Bagchi from Charles.

'You're friends with a terrorist?' She asked in disgust.

Bagchi took a deep breath and said, 'I am a businessman, Mr Brown, and I have many friends, but let me assure you Khan is not one of them.' 'Thank God you're not his friend. He is a terrorist and a perpetrator.' Charles remarked.

'Well, Mr Brown, we are intelligent people, and there is no reason for us to associate with someone like Khan.' He gave a sly grin. Charles seemed impressed with Bagchi, whom he had once considered imperious and belligerent. He had fulfilled his promise and got the necklace Charles so desperately wanted. 'I should have brought you the deal. It seems our middleman was insignificant after all.' Charles remarked.

Both the men laughed at their accomplishment and shook hands affably before bidding farewell. 'All this for an exhibition?' Firdaus asked in exasperation as they exited the room.

'I don't get how an intelligent woman like you can be so naive?' Bagchi asked as they made their way out of the building. 'What do you mean?' She stopped walking. 'I mean, no one ever pays so much to display what they've got. Charles will sell the necklace to the highest bidder in the auction that'll take place after the exhibition.' Firdaus looked at him with shock.

'I can't believe you sold the most precious treasure to someone like him.'

'My ethics are convoluted.' He retorted.

He gazed at Firdaus's shirt, which had this button that reflected sunlight, whereas the others looked opaque. He stared at it for a few moments. 'Where is your black sedan?' She asked.

'We're taking the train.' He responded, still staring at the button. Then he looked up and smiled. 'Shall we go?'

His sharp jawline looked a little sterner & grimmer as he settled on the chair opposite Firdaus. 'Where are we going?' She snapped. 'It was a pleasure working with you.' He said with a smile. 'Now, it's time for you to reunite with your daughter.'

Firdaus's face was unable to bear her unfeigned joy. 'Where is she?' She asked, almost choking on emotions. 'She is sitting near the window in the third compartment.' Firdaus thought her body jerked with excitement, but it was the train that had moved from the station. She got up from her chair to rush to her daughter, but Bagchi grabbed her arm and pulled her towards him before she could move. He smelled her cologne by bringing his mouth near her neck.

'What are you doing?' She asked in distress.

He brought his mouth near her collar and moved it towards her button. 'Whoever is listening, I have a deal for you.' He whispered. Firdaus stood rock-still with a brooding silence and later sank into her seat.

'How did you know?' She muttered.

'I have many talents; one of them is excellent observational skill. So, tell me, was that necklace real or...? 'It was a replica.' She admitted before he could finish his sentence. 'Great, now I want you to call your agent.' He demanded. 'What's your deal.' A woman's voice came through the phone. 'You give me a safe passage to India, and in return, I'll tell you where Karim Khan is.' Bagchi proposed his deal confidently.

'How do we know you're giving us the right location?' Maria asked in her perfectly balanced voice. 'I have no reason to lie. He is a bigger threat to me right now than you.' His voice was earnest. After a few seconds of contemplation, she replied, 'you got yourself a deal Bagchi. Well played.'

'Now, can I please see my daughter?' Firdaus lunged out of her seat.

'You sure can. You're free to go.' He replied with a smile. At that moment, she felt like killing him and taking her vengeance for the misery he had caused. Her rage had captivated her mind, and she had almost raised her fist to smack his head but then realized getting Ariana back was more important to her. The next station is Waterloo - an announcement echoed in the compartment, making many passengers get up from their seats and surround the door. As the train came to a halt, Firdaus scurried out of the train and rushed to the third compartment. 'Ariana, Aru..' She called. She hurried across the compartment to find her daughter and saw a little girl sitting in a window seat next to her caretaker. She was holding a doll in her hands and was squeezing it tight as if she would never let her go. 'Aru, my love.' Her eyes sparkled with unshed tears.

'Mom,' Ariana jumped from her seat and ran to her. 'I missed you so much. 'Her innocent voice pierced her heart. 'I missed you too, my love, but don't worry, I am here now.' She hugged her tight.

'Firdaus', Maria called from behind. She turned around and said furiously, 'you let him go.' Maria remained silent. 'You freed the man who kidnapped a 4-year-old girl and not just any girl, your granddaughter. Good job.' She jibed.

'Karim is a bigger threat, Firdaus. Once we have him, I promise Bagchi will pay for what he has done.'

'I don't believe you.' Firdaus scoffed. The little girl standing between her mother's two feet with her hands wrapped around her waist turned around and asked, 'who is she, mom?'

Maria knelt to match the height of the little one and placed her hand on her cheek. 'My name is Maria, and I am...' She looked at Firdaus to answer that question. 'She is my friend.' Firdaus replied.

Ariana smiled and then looked towards her mother. 'I want an ice -cream. Can we please get ice cream?' The child demanded.

'I think I should go.' Maria got up on her feet again. 'I'll see you at the hotel. Firdaus nodded.

'What ice cream do you want, Aru? Firdaus asked, walking towards the escalator.

'I want vanilla and blueberry.' The child grinned.

Suddenly, the station plunged into chaos as the crowd from one particular compartment of the train jumped out on the platform, pushing open the automatic door. Something had created confusion and panic aboard the train and inside the station.

Firdaus clung to Ariana as the frenzied passengers ran past them. A tall man in a black hoodie had nestled the gun barrel between Bagchi's eyes.

'You betrayed me, and you know how much I frown upon betrayal.' Said the man. Bagchi's eyes widened with fear. 'You!' His body shivered frantically. 'How did you know I was here?' He stammered as his throat swelled in fear.

'Why did you betray me?'

'I didn't want to, but you left me with no choice. You are delusional! You think you can launch a nuclear weapon on India. It is impossible.'

Khan pressed the barrel deeper into his forehead. 'Where is the woman who found the necklace?' He asked grimly.

Debojeet moved his eyes to the window opposite him through which he could see Firdaus standing with her daughter. He raised his arm to point at her, and that's when the black hoodie pressed the trigger, driving the bullet straight into his skull.

Firdaus pulled Ariana towards her and turned the little girl's face to her belly. The black hoodie quickly darted to the window to see what Bagchi pointed at before dying. He gave a death stare to Firdaus, who froze like a statue, watching Bagchi die in front of her eyes. As the black hoodie motioned towards the door, Firdaus held Ariana's hand and said, 'baby, you want to stay with Mumma, right?' The girl nodded in fear. 'Then you must do as I say.' The tall man walked through the crowd to where Firdaus was standing. She brought her mouth chillingly close to the little girl's ear and said, 'run'.

* * *

Maria had transformed her hotel room into her personal operational space. Her agents were busy answering the phones that consistently rang when the news of Karim Khan being in London was aired. Mihir zoomed in on the subway map on his laptop leading from Piccadilly Circus to Lambeth North, assuming Karim would have boarded the train from Waterloo and killed Bagchi in Lambeth North. Aryan paced the room, worrying about Firdaus and his daughter at Lambeth North when Bagchi was murdered.

Mihir informed Maria that the local authorities had sent the CCTV footage, and it was ready if she wanted to take a look. Maria lunged to her laptop to play the footage but got distracted when someone stomped on the door. She opened the door and found Firdaus standing with her chin down and shoulder hunched as if she was defeated on a battlefield but had returned alive.

'I was so worried for you.' Maria hugged her.

Firdaus stood there with her hands hung loose and face as stiff as marble. Aryan kissed her cheek and said, 'thank God you're alright.'

'He took her'. She said, sinking into the chair. 'What do you mean?' Mihir brought her a glass of water. 'Ariana ran as much as she could, but someone pushed me, and my hand slipped from hers. She looked up to Aryan in tears and said, 'she fell on the ground.' Firdaus yowled in grief.

'He caught her and took her with him. I couldn't do anything.' Aryan's face turned red with the blood that rushed to his cheeks.

'I'll kill him if he lays a hand on my daughter.' His voice roared like a tiger. Maria called her friend in MI6 to inform him that Karim had managed to escape with a four-year-old girl. Immediately after her phone call, the local police and MI6 told the civil aviation authorities to watch for a potential terrorist on the flight and also warned the train transport services to keep an eye out for a tall Arab man in a black hoodie.

'Calm down, Firdaus.' Maria patted her consolingly on the shoulder. 'I'll get your daughter back.' Firdaus dropped herself into her arms and pleaded, 'please get her back. I can't live without her.' Maria wiped her tears and said, 'I promise you, I'll not let anything happen to that girl.'

'Maria, we missed him.' Audrey, the MI6 agent, said on the phone.

'What do you mean?' Maria asked.

'He crossed the border. He is in Paris right now. Oh no, wait, he is on his way to Istanbul.' Audrey corrected herself when she heard the latest update from another agent keeping track of his movements.

'Are you sure this is our man?'

'Yes, he boarded the flight with a four-year-old.' She replied.

'Oh, damn it!' Maria hung up and threw her phone on the bed.

'What happened?' Aryan anxiously strode to her.

'We lost him.'

'Fuck....', she yelled, clenching her teeth.

'So, what are we going to do now?' Asked Mihir.

Maria took two deep breaths to get her composure back, and once she felt both her breath and temper under control, she said, 'you must go to Istanbul.'

'I'll come with you.' Aryan volunteered.

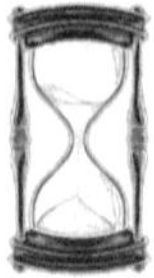

Chapter 12

Istanbul, Turkey

Aryan stifled his urge to cry as he sat on the bench facing the sea of Marmara. He looked anguished, agitated and on the cusp of breaking down. His overwhelming rage made him want to burn and destroy anything that stood against him and his daughter, but all he managed to do was exhale a sigh that sounded more like a grunt. He took his wallet and pulled out a photograph from it. Ariana's innocent smile melted his heart, and before he knew it, the corners of his mouth rose to form a smile. 'Look at her,' he said to Mihir. 'Her eyes, her smile, she is just like me, isn't she?' Mihir smiled and nodded. 'We'll find her soon, brother. Don't worry.'

The hunched-back Turkish tea stall owner kept the double-stacked teapot on the stove and waited for the flame to cradle it. After a few minutes, when the pungent aroma filled his nostrils, he turned off the stove and poured the piping hot black tea into two tulip-shaped glasses for the gentlemen sitting on the bench. Mihir took two sips of the tea and stepped aside to make a call. When he returned, Aryan had left the bench. Mihir looked around for him and saw his friend standing against an ice-cream cart. He bought an ice-cream cone for the child who held his hand. He gave the cone to the child and gently kissed his forehead. The child took the ice cream and darted to his mother, who stood on the corner of the footpath. Her tunic was covered in dust and stinking, and her bowl had a few coins she would probably use to buy bread for her son. Aryan took off his leather jacket and offered it to the poor lady who was shivering in the cold.

Aryan's soul was tattered by the cruel hands of fate. His heart was aching for the child he had never met. The absence from his daughter's life gnawed at his soul. The ache of not witnessing her birth and her growth was haunting him. In that very moment, he cursed Firdaus for not telling him about the existence of Ariana before. Every little boy or girl on the street stirred memories of his estranged daughter, whose photo was the only thing he had of hers.

Mihir grabbed Aryan and said, 'Listen, we need to go.' Aryan looked at him with tears in his eyes. 'What happened?' 'We need to find her as soon as possible. She is kept somewhere against her will, probably terrified and traumatised. I need to find her and bring her back. He said wearily.

'Don't worry, we will. Farooq Siddiqui is going to help us find her.'

'Who is he?'

'He is an Indian agent posing as a Syrian refugee. He has many contacts and knows people who could help us. 'Do you know where to find him?' 'We'll find him at the Grand Bazar.' Said Mihir, getting the confirmation from a source of his.

The market sprawled from west to east between two mosques. Throbbing with locals and tourists, that bazaar was absolutely chaotic. The shop owners were loud and shouted ridiculously discounted prices to attract tourists. The murmuring sounds that came from the corner coffee shop were a mix of different languages and accents. These voices, together with the yelling of the store owners, echoed in the enclosed space and created a cacophony that would buzz in one's ear even after they left the place.

Mihir unlocked his phone and showed the picture of the man they were looking for to the owner of an antique shop. 'Have you seen this man?' He asked, pointing his finger to the picture on the phone. The store owner nodded no. They moved on to the next shop that displayed a variety of spices strong enough to flare their nostrils. Mihir asked the same question to the owner, and he nodded as well. They moved from shop to shop, asking people if they knew Farooq. They all denied. Then there was this jeweller who sent them off pretending not to know or understand their language, but when they left, he made a suspicious call to someone.

'No one knows Farooq. This is unbelievable. Mihir said, gulping solid Turkish coffee from a tiny cup. 'Are you sure we'll find him here?'

'I am positive. Our intel is hardly wrong.' He convinced himself. Aryan glanced through the stores on the opposite side. The textile stall had maximum visitors, trying on Ottoman caps & cashmere scarfs. The ceramic alcove next to it had plenty of tourists looking at the mosaic lamps and Turkish glassware. Then there was a spice seller who had laid out all the fragrant & colourful spices in a pyramid shape. Although that spice stall had everything to impress a passer-by, it lacked customers. The short man got up from his chair and glared at Aryan with his pale blue eyes. Aryan strode to him to know the reason for his fury, but before he could speak to him, the blue-eyed man took out a knife from his pocket and pointed the steel blade at him.

'What do you want from Farooq?' He asked from his clenched teeth. Mihir punched the short man from the side, smashing his cheek on the spice tray. The short man howled in pain as he staggered back, half his face covered in sumac. A kick on his gut made him stomp on the ground. Aryan pressed his foot on his hand, making it impossible for him to move his finger and then snatched the knife from him. Mihir pulled his collar to get him up on his feet.

'How do you know Farooq? Where is he?' He growled. The short man raised his ravaged eyes to meet Mihir's. The man's unnerving glare forced him to reveal the reason for initiating a brawl. Before he could say something, another man attacked Mihir, striking him down with a cane. Within seconds, Aryan found himself surrounded by two more men who came with the attacker. 'What do you want?' Aryan cried. None of them answered. The bald-headed man moved forward and punched his jaw with his fist. Aryan's head whipped back as he stumbled. He pushed the man away from him to gain a brief respite.

Mihir shuddered out of concussion and struggled to get up. Aryan offered his hand to bring him up to his feet, and the two men advanced with an unnerving speed. Mihir smacked a ceramic pot on his attacker's bald head, and Aryan strangled the tall one with a pashmina hanging outside the textile stall. The bald head recoiled and fell. Blood rushed from his nose. As the tall man struggled to breathe, he grabbed a souvenir from the display and scratched Aryan's arms with it to loosen his grip. Aryan snarled and smacked his head into a glass cabinet.

Mihir arched backwards when the spice seller tried to strike again with a knife. He knelt and slid from between his legs. He lunged and kicked the seller's butt, making him fall to the ground. The third guy nervously watched his friends getting beaten up but could not gather the courage to face the enraged men.

The emerging stubble covering parts of his jawline proved he was not a year more than in his late teens. He was probably promised a packet of cigarettes or a bottle of his favourite beer in exchange for this fight. He wanted to do his job, but not at the cost of broken bones. He sweated profusely when he saw both the men coming forth. He pulled out a small pistol from his back pocket and pointed it toward the two men.

'Stop.' He howled. 'Don't move, or I'll shoot.'

'You don't have to do this?' Mihir took a step forward cautiously.

'I said, don't move.' The boy took a step back.

'Tell me, what do you want from Farooq?'

'We just want to talk. We have come all the way from India.' Aryan answered.

The assembled crowd hooted at the sight of a gun. The women and children screamed in fear, and the men in fury.

A tall and muscular man emerged from the crowd and stood between the guy with the gun and the two men. 'It's okay. I'll take it from here.' He signalled the boy to lower his weapon. The boy's eyes flickered with trepidation. He glanced at Mihir and Aryan and then at the man standing ahead. He finally dropped his arms and said, 'yes, sir.' The man turned around and offered a handshake. 'I am Farooq Siddiqui. I hear you're looking for me.'

'We must talk in private.' Mihir insisted.

'You must first tell me what you want?' Farooq asked.

'We need your help to find my daughter.' Farooq took a few minutes to contemplate and then agreed.

'I'll meet you at Cafe Marmara in Taksim Square fifteen minutes from now.'

Farooq didn't wait for their reaction. He turned around and walked deeper into the market until he dispersed in the crowd.

Café Marmara was a kebab eatery. A small restaurant in the crowded Taksim Square. Farooq always preferred to meet agents in a crowded space. After meeting Aryan and Mihir, Farooq's thoughts were a tangle of curiosity and apprehension. He wanted to help them but did not trust them enough, so he thought a crowded place like Taksim Square was an excellent spot to meet the gentlemen. Worst case, if it turns out to be a trap, he would use the crowd as his shield and vanish without leaving a trace. He thought. When he arrived, Mihir asked, 'What was the need for a fight?

'Many people come looking for me. I just wanted to make sure you were indeed Indian agents.'

'Well, now you know.' He sighed, placing the ice pack on the back of his head.

'We're looking for Karim Khan. He came to Istanbul the day before yesterday and has been in exile ever since.'

'He has my daughter.' Aryan said drearily.

'Why Istanbul? When he can go anywhere in the world.' Farooq muttered.

'Probably, he has friends here who would protect him.'

'Or he has come to make a deal,' Farooq interfered.

'What kind of deal?'

'The kind that destroys peace in the world.'

'What do you mean?'

'I've received intel suggesting there's a clandestine arms transaction in the works, involving an Arab businessman and Istanbul's leading weapon manufacturer, Ahmet Aydin. A source of mine disclosed this to me a few weeks back, affirming Aydin's pursuit for a valuable treasure that could potentially bring chaos in the East.'

'If your information is true, we must haste.' Said Mihir.

'Oh no, there is no way we can walk into any of Aydin's facilities. All his warehouses are heavily guarded. And even if we succeed in sneaking in, we would be outnumbered by his loyal army.'

'We cannot just sit here. We must do something.' Aryan threw his arm in the air out of frustration.

'We will.' Mihir declared.

'How?' Farooq arched one of his eyebrows.

'By pretending to be employees.' He replied.

The three men sought employment opportunities at one of Ahmet's warehouses, the one that accepted refugees. Since Farooq lived locally, he had learnt the language and had become resourceful over time. He told the manager that he had found the two men he was accompanying at a Syrian refugee camp. He pleaded on behalf of the men to give them employment, pointing out that the guys had not eaten in days and were looking for a job to feed them and their families. They were immediately employed and soon given a position of preparing weapon consignments for Ahmet's clients.

Farooq had volunteered to deliver these consignments to the buyers as he knew the city well and could speak Turkish fluently. Making a few trips to Ahmet's other locations, Farooq had learnt almost everything there was to know about the business and the clientele. He would come back and tell the boys about the security at every facility and the number of men guarding it. Mihir and Aryan had made a few friends who could speak English. They learned from them that a big meeting was supposed to happen in a few days between Ahmet and the Arab businessman. It was the same information that Farooq had passed on. Mihir was sure the Arab man was none other than Karim Khan. He immediately made a call to Maria to inform her of their findings. On that call, she told them she had a plan and was about to execute it soon. Upon learning that the boys had access to Aydin's facilities, she had advised them to look for proof that leads them to their guy. 'Find the smoke, and you'll know where the fire is.' She said before hanging up.

During one of Farooq's trips, he had seen Ahmet talking to a wrinkled guy that matched the description of the man Mihir and

Aryan were looking for. Karim was sitting with Ahmet in his office, a glass cubicle in the middle of the warehouse. Farooq hid behind his truck and took pictures of both the men. He went back and showed it to the boys. Mihir's eyes had widened in surprise. 'Good god. We found him.' Aryan felt rage rising within him as he looked at the photo. 'Yes, he is the one.' He snarled.

Chapter 13

London, 2 Days Ago

Maria waited until after the auction started before slipping into the National Gallery. She had ordered the police to stay close and bust in when she signalled. The auction was organised explicitly for guests with high net worth and elite social standing. All the seats were reserved for invitation-only guests. The VIPs had already settled with their boastful purses and fancy placards. Maria took a spot in the rear corner near the stone pillar that supported the vaulted ceiling to avoid being seen or recognised.

The auction had begun, and two items were sold already. Maria glanced at the room, looking for exits that people might use to run upon the arrival of the police. 'There are two exits.' She whispered on her handheld radio. 'I want five men covering the west gate and five near the south gate.'

'The next item on display is an epitome of elegance and decadence. This century-old necklace is designed by Cartier for the Prince of Patiala. This marvel from India is worth 100 million dollars. So, we start the bid at $101.' The auctioneer announced. Three bids came almost immediately, but all low, the last at 110 million dollars. Charles looked ecstatic, gloating about his successful discovery. He whispered something to one of his guests, and the guest raised the bid to $130 million. The lady in the third row called a bid for 150 million dollars. Charles' guest, sitting in the first row, turned his head to the lady. He seemed perturbed by the unexpected challenge and upped his bid to 170 million dollars. Others sensed the worth of the necklace by mere competition and raised the offer to 200 million dollars. After almost five minutes of intense bidding, Maria rose from her seat and called out a bid for 500 million dollars.

The room fell silent, and all heads turned to her at once. 'The current bid is at $500 million. Do we have any more bids?' The auctioneer announced. No one dared to raise their placard. Charles kept his gaze intact at the lady in the white dress, who had called for a bid that no one could catch up to. 'The necklace is sold to the lady in white for 500 million dollars.' The auctioneer retrieved the necklace from the easel and placed it back into the velvet box. Maria came forth and asked the auctioneer to step aside. She took the mic and made the announcement.

'Ladies and gentlemen, the beautiful necklace Mr Charles has been boasting about the entire evening belongs to my country and shall remain there. However, this necklace introduced to you as the great Patiala necklace is fake and not even worth 1000 dollars.' The revelation shocked the crowd. Charles looked flustered and held his chest like he was going to have a stroke. 'The necklace you all were about to spend millions of dollars on is sadly fake. So, you're welcome. And yes, Mr Charles Brown, you're under arrest for auctioning government-owned art & antiques. The police busted in, and before Charles had the time to react, he was handcuffed and dragged out of the building. The scattered crowd strode for the exit, hardly knowing both the doors were guarded by the police waiting for them to come out. Their eyes squinted from the flashlights of the cameras, and ears numbed from the shrill voices of the reporters. Soon every TV and newspaper broadcasted the news of the illegal auction that sold antiques worth millions of dollars, including the replica of the Patiala necklace. Many internet sleuths posted articles and blogs on the fake Necklace being auctioned. They came up with their own theories regarding the disappearance and whereabouts of the original Patiala necklace.

Firdaus lay on the couch in agony. She crumbled as she wept. 'Aru....' she cried, 'why her?' Why do you have to make her suffer? 'She looked up in the air as if she was talking to God.' I have never asked you for anything, have I? You took away my family, my friends, even the love of my life, but I lived, I carried on.' Her cheeks were damp, and her eyes red from lack of sleep.

Her soliloquy would have lasted longer if her phone hadn't rung. She pushed the green button and held the phone to her ear. 'Firdaus.' A deep voice came through. She jumped off the couch. 'Who is this? 'Her voice was raspy from all the crying and weeping. 'I have your daughter.' She trembled. 'You know what you must do if you want to see her alive.' The man's voice was fierce and rigid, unlike Bagchi's. Firdaus wasn't sure if Bagchi was capable of harming her daughter, but she knew Karim was not only capable but also willing. He had been deceived and hurt; more importantly, he was a devil in the face of humanity. She couldn't take any risk with him. 'I'll get you the necklace. Please don't hurt her.' She pleaded. 'I want it by tomorrow.' He sounded serious. 'Tomorrow.' Firdaus's voice sounded skeptical. 'Yes.'

'Okay, where should I bring it?' 'To Istanbul, and yes, you dare inform the police. I'll... 'No, please, you don't have to threaten me. I won't tell anyone.' Firdaus cut him off. 'I am glad to hear. See you soon, Ms Durrani.'

* * *

Mihir and Aryan found a spot to hide behind the trailer carrying weapons to the warehouse. One man was unloading the containers from the trailer, and the other two who accompanied him were taking them to their designated places. Ahmet's glass office was just ten metres away from the boys. Yet, they stayed put, fearful of being caught by the two men guarding the office and the three men unloading weapons across from it.

Ahmet had established a strict rule of not letting his employees wander around in places where they were not needed. Everyone was handed a list of tasks every morning, and they were only supposed to attend to that. Mihir and Aryan had received their duties, and those tasks did not involve being around Ahmet's office. They were not even supposed to be at that warehouse. But they hid behind the trailer, waiting for their chance to enter the glass cubicle. When the two men finished unloading, they moved the truck with the trailer on the side. The boys had managed to jump inside the trailer. They had covered themselves with the jute bags and laid straight on their backs as the truck moved on the side. When the driver left, they jumped out of the vehicle and crept to the electrical panel. Aryan pulled the switches down, and the warehouse turned dark. They had come unplanned and were acting out of instinct. There was only plan A, and that was to search Ahmet's office to find a clue of the location their boss had chosen for his meeting with the Arab businessman. Their plan B involved saving themselves from being caught. They could not take that chance, at least not before they had fulfilled the purpose of the visit.

The guard flinched as the light from two torches flashed on his face. 'Do you know what's wrong with the electricity?' A voice came from behind the torch. The guard nodded no. 'I don't know. There must be an outage.' 'You must go and check. If the boss comes to know about this. He'll not be happy.' The guard did not recognise the voice. 'Who are you? 'He asked. 'We are the men who unloaded the weapons.' Aryan replied. ' We would have checked for the fault, but we don't know where the panel is.' Said Mihir. 'Can you guard the office until we return? The guard asked. The boys nodded and took their spots.

When the guards left, they switched off their torch and entered the office. 'How will we do this without the torch?' Aryan whispered. 'Don't worry, I got this.' Mihir replied. 'Just stay at the door and turn on your phone torchlight.' Aryan stood at the door and turned his phone light towards the wooden desk. 'Don't flash the light directly. Just hold it straight.' 'You won't have much visibility.' 'That's okay. I'll manage.'

They did not have much time. It was a matter of minutes before someone would find out that the lights were switched off by someone and there was nothing wrong with the electricity. Mihir had to act fast. He had to unlock Ahmet's computer and get the information they were after before the lights were turned on again. He was a trained agent, and it wasn't challenging for him to work in the dark, but unlocking the computer was beyond his expertise. He tried punching some numbers and alphabets but failed to succeed. He banged on the table. 'What's wrong.' Aryan yelled. 'I can't crack the password.' He sighed. His fingers clenched the table's edge and accidentally pushed the lever underneath.

'What are we going to do now?' Aryan feared. Someone turned on the lights, and the guard returned to their spots. Aryan and Mihir looked at them in horror, but they appeared unperturbed. They took their spot facing the entrance of the warehouse. Aryan was perplexed. 'What just happened?' 'I think they didn't see us?' 'How come this is a glass office? 'Unless it's not?' 'What do you mean?' 'I accidentally pushed a lever. That might have made the glass opaque from outside.' 'Well, in that case, we're in luck. We have the whole night to unlock his computer.' Aryan grinned.

Mihir called their cyber expert in India and got him to unlock Ahmet's computer. He attached the pen drive he brought with him and copied all the data stored in Aydin's personal folders, including information on his deals, bank accounts, details of people on his hit list, everything. Mihir then opened his calendar and discovered that he had booked a private yacht for his meeting with Karim. The meeting was scheduled for noon on the next day. Mihir noted the address and turned off the computer. 'We'll have to spend the night here.' He told Aryan. 'This place is always guarded. There is no way we can exit without being noticed.' 'You're right.' Mihir kept the pen drive in his backpack and locked the chain. 'Then we're only left with one option.

We'll have to fight.

8 Hours Ago

Istiklal Street was crowded as usual. It was 11 am, and heaps of people, especially tourists, were busy shopping for souvenirs, drinking tea and coffee, chatting with their friends and enjoying the sun-drenched streets of Istanbul. Firdaus had arrived at the location with the necklace. She chose a spot outside a closed furniture shop in a slightly less crowded alleyway and waited for Karim to come. Maria ensured Firdaus was standing exactly where she was advised to by zooming her binoculars. She moved them slightly to the right to see the end of the street. Next to her was a man in a black leather jacket aiming his rifle at the spot opposite Firdaus. When he saw a man approaching her, he adjusted the optic on the rifle and aimed the gun at him. 'Don't shoot until I tell you to.' Maria ordered.

Firdaus had no option but to summon her inner resolve. She confidently faked her 'don't give a shit' attitude, masking any signs of nervousness and vulnerability. Ariana's safety was important to her, but her willingness to be flicked around by men like Karim Khan for their own cause had been demolished. Maria had informed her that Mihir and Aryan were sent after Ahmet Aydin, who had allegedly kept her abducted daughter in one of his facilities. Trusting Aryan to get their daughter back safely, she didn't care about herself and made it her life's mission to destroy Karim Khan.

She took a cigarette from the steel case she was carrying and stashed the case back into her pocket. She flicked the lighter and inhaled a drag. As the smoke floated through her dark pink lips, a temporary haze prevented her from seeing Karim's dark eyes glistening in the sunlight. 'This feels amazing. Having a smoke after so many days.' Karim Khan didn't answer. Cigarette dangling, Firdaus walked closer and looked straight into his eyes. 'I have what you want.' 'What is she doing?' Maria murmured. 'I don't have a clear aim. She needs to move back.' Said the sniper, adjusting the optic again. Karim's gaze was fixed on her. She whipped out the necklace from her purse and gave it to him. 'Where is my daughter?' She asked. 'She is not here.' Khan replied. She came closer to intimidate him. 'If you have harmed her in any way, I'll make your life a living hell.' Something touched her belly; it was a pistol. She stared up in terror as he shoved the barrel further into her skin. 'You won't do anything.' His evil eyes flashed anger.

'I have partial access to the target. Do you want me to shoot? The sniper turned his head to Maria and waited for her order. Maria adjusted her binoculars and zoomed in. 'Do not shoot until you have clear access. We don't want any civilian casualties.' Her tone was stern and rigid, like the tone of an agent in authority. But her heart was in shreds. She felt an acute pain that paralyzed her brain. The thought of her daughter dying in front of her eyes was unbearable. She wanted to save her and was determined to let go of Karim if it came to that.

Firdaus flinched. 'Don't shoot me, or you'll die.' You're lying.' 'No, I am not. A sniper is aiming at you right now. If you shoot me, he'll shoot you, and we both will die.' He moved his pistol away from her belly and pulled her towards him. Holding her by her waist, he aimed the gun at her temple and threatened to shoot. 'Show yourself, or I'll shoot her.' He yelled. Maria panicked. She rose up from behind the wall and raised her arms. 'Let her go.' A black Mercedes speeded into the alleyway and stopped outside the furniture shop. The driver unlocked the door, and before Maria could react, Karim fled with Firdaus.

Maria rushed to the street to stop the vehicle; her expression wrought with grief and panic. 'Firdaus', she called out and dropped to her knees on the road.

'Where are you taking me?' Firdaus cried. Karim sat comfortably on his seat as the car drove past the city and merged onto the main highway. Minutes later, he replied. 'I've heard you're lucky for men trying to crack a deal.' She didn't respond. 'You proved to be lucky for Bagchi. He got the necklace.' 'And then he got killed. So, I guess I am not that lucky after all.' 'It was his choice that got him killed, not his luck.' Firdaus looked away and stared at the window. 'You want to see your daughter alive, don't you? 'I know you'll kill me as soon as I am of no use to you.' She said blatantly. 'Don't give me false hopes.' 'You see, Firdaus, hope is a dangerous thing. It comes first and leaves last; sometimes, it doesn't leave at all. It is a delusion that keeps us going.' A moment of silence followed. 'I promise I won't kill you.' She looked into his eyes and was amazed by his earnestness. 'You took me with you at gunpoint, which means I'll have to do what you tell me to do anyway.' She was right. He did not have to promise her anything. 'I am not as bad as you think.' He explained. 'I don't care.' She looked away again. 'If I was a bad person, I would have killed your mother, you know.' She felt air rushing out of her lungs. 'What do you mean?' 'Firdaus, I know this is a fake necklace.' Both fell into silence for a while. 'I didn't punish you or her because I don't really care. As long as you convince my partner that this is the real necklace just the way you convinced Charles, I am happy to set you free and let you reunite with your daughter.' 'And why do you think he'll believe me?' 'Because you have exceptional manipulative skills! At least, that's what I have heard.'

'If I make this deal for you, you'll destroy my country.'

'That's true, Ms Durrani. Make a choice; you want to save your daughter or your country.'

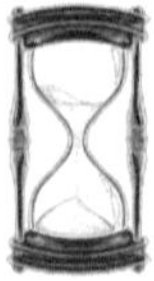

Chapter 14

Istanbul, Turkey

A sudden strike on the head and the guard fell to the ground to his stomach. Aryan had smacked him with a laptop, but before he could turn to the other guard, that other guard had raised his gun and fired a shot in Aryan's direction. The bullet pierced his shirt and hit his elbow. As he staggered in pain, the guard took the opportunity and attacked him from behind. Fuelled by rage, Mihir kicked the guard and gave him a couple of tough blows on his face until he lost his balance and dropped to the ground. The guard was wounded and hurt and yet was refusing to yield. He dragged himself towards the pistol that had fallen down when the other guard hit the ground, but before he could reach, Mihir struck him with a knife and shoved it deep into his shoulder until the tip of it hit the spine. Tossing him out, he moved towards Aryan. That poor guy was howling in pain when Mihir dressed his wound with a handkerchief.

The blaring siren had alarmed others in the warehouse. It was a sign of an emergency. They had picked up their weapons and were on the hunt for the boys. Aryan and Mihir made their way to the corner where machine guns, explosives and smoke bombs were stacked. They carried as many weapons as they could and strode towards the exit. As they got out of their cover, a firing session followed that left half a dozen men incapacitated.

Karim held Firdaus by her arm and dragged her to the yacht. 'I hope you have made your decision.' He said, tightening his grip around her arm. 'I'll help you.' Her heart sank as she uttered those words. Karim took his hand off her. 'Good, let's get this done. Shall we?'

The captain welcomed them on the yacht and ushered them to the deck where Ahmet was waiting. Karim stopped Firdaus in the middle. 'You must fix your hair and clothes before heading to the deck.' He ran his fingers through her hair and placed a strand behind her ear. 'Don't touch me.' She shrugged. Her tone was intense. Karim took his hand away. 'I am sorry.' 'Why are you doing this?' Tears covered her eyes. 'I am on a mission, like any other soldier.' 'You are not a soldier. You are a terrorist.' She shot back. Karim sighed. 'Revolution comes at a cost. You'll not understand because you've not faced what I have. So, let's not waste any more time.' One last look into her eyes, and Karim turned around to walk towards the deck.

She combed her hair and tied them into a low bun. Her face looked pale and bloodless in the mirror. She had not eaten properly for days and had barely slept. She looked terrible. Firdaus turned on the tap and splashed cold water on her face. What had to be done had to be done. There wasn't another way. She thought.

She unzipped her purse and whipped out a lip gloss and a compact powder from her makeup bag. With a bit of touch-up, she was herself again. Karim and Ahmet raised their glass of champagne to celebrate their victory. She couldn't stand that sight. She did her best to control her urge to kill them. Many different ways to finish them struck her brain, but none seemed achievable. She felt dizzy from all the thoughts that raced through her mind. She had to stop them, and there was literally no time to think. Firdaus closed her eyes to gain some respite. As her eyelids fell, her past flashed across her eyes and reminded her of that one thing that always worked in her favour. Deceiving them both was her endgame!

In life, there comes a pivotal moment when all that you know and believe in is put to the ultimate test and for Firdaus, this was that moment. She knew failing in her plan could bring grave danger not only to herself but also to her daughter. She weighed the risks and the potentials outcomes of those risks in her mind and yet resolved to proceed with her plan regardless.

Ahmet's army consisted of trained men who could fight and kill. Aryan and Mihir had the weapons, but they were two against many. They had to come up with a combat plan to save themselves from being killed. As they advanced to the exit door, Mihir shot five men who aimed at them from the first floor, and Aryan killed the two who attacked from behind. He plunged the knife into their stomach and drilled it deeper until they sprawled on the ground. Mihir hid behind the pillar and continued firing. A strong and forceful slam on the head and Aryan fell to the floor.

His eyes flickered as he tried to hold his consciousness. A muscular man had knocked him down by hitting his head with the back of his gun. Before Aryan could move, he was above his chest, with one knee to his heart and the other pushing his palm. He tried to choke him by pressing his neck with his hands. Aryan coughed and gasped for air. Mihir saw him and got out of his spot to help, but two gunshots toward him, and he was back behind the pillar again. Aryan's one hand was wounded, and the other stuck under the muscular man's knee. He had no choice but to move his leg. He made a futile effort to rise up using the power of his feet, but the muscular man on top weighed more than him, and he stopped his movement by tightening his grip even more against his neck.

His intention was not to kill him but to make him unconscious until he knocked down the second man (Mihir). His orders were to keep them alive until Ahmet came back. Aryan was almost unconscious but could partially see someone coming toward the muscular man. The person behind him swung the rod and shattered his skull with it. His head fell on Aryan's chest. Aryan moved the hands that enclosed his neck and got up, breathing erratically. He rubbed his eyes to clear his vision. A petite woman with thick glasses stood against him. She seemed to want to scream, but fear quelled her voice. Her hands were still shaking out of nervousness.

'Who are you? What are you doing here?' Aryan pulled her to the side behind another pillar to save her from the gunshots coming his way. 'I... I' She couldn't let the words out of her mouth. 'Don't be scared.' Tell me who you are? She didn't reply. 'Do you speak in English?' She nodded. 'Very little.' Aryan asked her what she was doing there using hand signs. 'Little girl. I... nanny'. The woman tried to explain. 'Little girl?' Aryan's heart skipped a beat. 'What girl?' He took a photo of his daughter from his wallet and showed it to her. 'This girl?' 'Yes.' The woman replied.

Ahmet stared at the stones that sparkled in the sunlight. He moved his gaze from the necklace to Firdaus and back to the Necklace again. 'I hope you liked it?' Karim looked straight into his eyes. 'It is the most beautiful thing I have ever seen.'

He touched the necklace. 'So, let's shake hands and seal the deal?' 'Absolutely.' He grinned. They got up from their seats and hugged each other. Firdaus wanted to rat him out and tell Ahmet that Karim had been lying to him and that the necklace was fake. However, she held her silence while the men exchanged gratitude and complemented each other out of mutual admiration.

A phone call distracted Ahmet, and he left the conversation abruptly. It was a call from one of his men from the warehouse. The frenzied caller told him about what was happening at the warehouse and that Aryan and Mihir had stolen his weapons and were now attacking his men. 'I am not worried about the weapons; they shouldn't get to the child. Make sure of that.' Anger and concern were felt in his voice. 'Stop them. Now!'

'It's over now. Just relax!' Firdaus gazed at the open sea across from her. 'I'll take you to your daughter.' Karim promised. She glared at him and moved her eyes to the sea again. 'Firdaus. There is no point sulking over something that's done. I must say you made a wise choice. Anyone in your situation would have done the same. So, don't beat yourself up unnecessarily.' Firdaus turned her head to Karim and saw Ahmet returning to the deck from behind. Since Karim was standing against her, he couldn't see Ahmet, but she could. 'He'll come to know that the necklace is fake, one way or the other, and he won't forgive us.' She raised her for Ahmet to hear. 'Don't worry about that.' He stood there calmly; Firdaus casually glanced to see if Ahmet was close enough to hear them. 'What you have done is despicable. You not only killed Debojeet for the fake necklace but tortured my daughter and blackmailed me into cheating Ahmet. All this for what? Karim looked grim. 'All this is for a cause.' He took a moment before continuing, 'my dream's going to come true. I'll set your capital city on fire.

It'll burn until the air becomes smoke, and the sky turns to a red cascade. That will be my ultimate revenge.'

Ahmet pulled out his gun and pointed the barrel at Karim. His eyes flashed fire. He couldn't bear the sight of the man who almost betrayed him. 'Ahmet, don't shoot. I can explain.' Karim raised his arms. The jumpy waves swayed the yacht, and everyone on it staggered for a moment. Ahmet held the railing of the boat with one hand while the other held onto the gun. Panic spread through Karim; he saw through Ahmet and knew he would shoot him regardless of his explanation. He could see rage rising within him, the kind of anger he had when he shot Bagchi. In the world of crime, the cost of betrayal was death. He had almost accepted his destiny and was ready to submit to death, but one giant wave and the gun Ahmet carried slipped from his hand and slid towards Karim. Firdaus plunged and caught the gun before Karim could get it. 'I'll shoot you both.' She yelled, swaying the gun from Ahmet to Karim.

'Where is my daughter?' She roared. 'Firdaus, don't be crazy. Just put down the gun.' Karim motioned towards Firdaus. She fired a warning shot to stop him. Upon hearing the gunshot, the captain rushed to the deck and tried to stop Firdaus from firing another. Firdaus aimed the gun at him, too, and threatened to shoot. 'I have your daughter. If you want to see her, you'll have to let me go.' Ahmet motioned in another direction to distract her, moved his finger in a circle twice, and opened his palm. This was a sign for the captain. While Firdaus and Karim had their eyes glued to Ahmet, the captain got his order and rushed back to his cabin.

A thick, oily object that smelt like kerosene spread through the deck. Firdaus felt her legs sticking to the floor as she tried to move backwards. Ahmet lunged forward and grabbed the gun from her hand. A strong punch followed, and she dropped to the ground. Blood splashed out of her mouth as her face hit the oily floor. 'You're a foolish woman. You all are useless.' He snorted and fired two shots at Karim. One hit his shoulder, and another pierced through his stomach. Karim screamed as the bullets wounded him. His hand lashed out at anything he could grasp, but nothing came forth, and he fell to the ground, gasping for air. Moments later, Firdaus opened her eyes and found herself tied to the railing. Karim lay still on the surface across from her, and Ahmet stood on the edge of the deck. He dropped the flickering lighter and set the boat ablaze. As the yacht burned, he jumped on a private boat that had come to pick him up and escaped.

Mihir and Aryan, along with the petite woman, were now in the backyard of the warehouse. They rushed to the shed attached to the parking lot and knocked down the door. Upon seeing them, Ariana dragged herself back from where she was sitting and clung to the wall. 'I want my mom,' she cried. She shivered with fear when she saw the gun in Mihir's hand. 'Please don't kill me.' She spoke nervously. Mihir dropped the gun. 'we're here to save you.' He said. Aryan kept staring at her. He was distraught. 'We'll take you to your mother.' Mihir offered his hand for her to grab. She didn't move and kept staring at the boys. Mihir looked at Aryan and said, 'I think you should try.' Aryan didn't move but kept looking at the girl. She looked just like him besides her brown eyes and long hair, which was like her mother's. Aryan took small steps towards her, keeping his gaze intact. He held her little hands and said, 'I know you're scared. But don't worry. I am here now.' 'I want my Mumma.' The little girl whispered. 'I promise you; I'll take you to her.' When she looked convinced, Aryan swaddled her in a blanket and picked her up in his arms.

The flame crackled around the boat, and the charcoaled smoke drifted into the haze. The fire had engulfed almost half of the yacht, and the other half had started crumbling. Only a few moments were left before an explosion would destroy the yacht entirely. Firdaus twisted her wrists to loosen the grip of the rope, but it stayed entangled around her hand. She tried again, now more vigorously, but her tied hands only slid from one side to another. She leaned forward, trying to reach for her feet, which were tied too. She could see the fire slowly gushing towards her and knew she only had a moment or two before she would burn and sink with the yacht. A faint voice of coughing came from her left and she looked at Karim. He was alive! His fingers moved first, then his palm and slowly his arms, he stretched it towards Firdaus. 'Please help me.' He pleaded.

Firdaus dragged her body and slid her hands on the railing towards her left. 'I'll help you, but first, you have to help me.' She said. Here, open my ropes.' She stretched her legs until her feet reached Karim. When Firdaus felt the rope slip through her ankles, she pulled the rope from her wrist to her mouth and used her feet to loosen it and teeth to untie it. Watching Karim in pain, she removed her scarf and tied it around his wound and hurried to the edge to look for a piece of wood that would allow Karim to float until help arrived. When she couldn't find anything, she turned around and looked into the eyes of the man who had kidnapped her daughter and had caused her days of misery. She saw through him and realized he wasn't worth saving. If she let him die today, she would only do a favour to the millions of people who would suffer if he got off the boat alive. 'Please, Firdaus, do something.' She ignored his plea. 'You dreamt of burning millions of people alive. What makes you think you deserve to live?' 'Please don't do this, Firdaus, save me; I promise I'll protect you and your family forever. I'll be indebted to you.' Two giant waves splashed cold water on his wounds and knocked him unconscious.

Firdaus dived into the sea and swam almost half a mile away from the boat. A big explosion crumbled the yacht, and pieces of the vessel sank into the sea.

* * *

A few days later....

Ariana grabbed a piece of bread from her mother's hand and fed it to the birds. The live music on the beach lifted her spirit, and she twirled and danced to the tune. Firdaus and Aryan watched the sea in silence, trying to fathom the past two weeks that changed their lives forever. 'Mom, look who is here!' Ariana said, holding Maria's hand. Firdaus turned. 'I didn't know you were still here.' Maria brought gifts for Ariana, gave them to the little girl, and walked towards Firdaus.

'I had asked her to stay.' Aryan said.

'Did you bring what I asked?'

'Yes.' Maria took out an envelope from her purse and gave it to Aryan. They shared a brief smile, and then he left to play with Ariana, leaving Firdaus and Maria to talk in private.

'I want you and Ariana back.'

'It's not that easy.' Firdaus retorted.

'I know you're hurt, Firdaus. I know I am the one who caused you this pain. But I would like nothing more than this one chance to make things right with you.' Firdaus didn't say anything. So, Maria continued. 'I have lived without my family for many years, and I know you think that was my choice, but I am only human. I make mistakes and leaving you was my biggest one.'

'I have made many mistakes myself, mother. I know I am flawed, and you are, too, but I would never let go of my daughter. She means everything to me. If you don't feel the same way for your daughter, then you and I are not alike.

'I love you a lot, my child. I do. Believe me.' Firdaus turned her gaze away from her mother.

'It is not about believing you; it is about trusting you. And I don't trust you.'

They both remained silent for a bit to let the tension wear out.

'Will you ever forgive me?' Tears demeaned her eyes.

'Maybe one day, but I won't keep you away from Ariana. You're free to visit her whenever you want.' Maria's hope to reunite with her girls surged when she heard her words. Her smile returned to her face.

'Thank you, Firdaus. Now, I must take your leave.' She planted a kiss on the little one's forehead before bidding her farewell. She wished Aryan the best of luck for his future and left.

Aryan handed Firdaus the envelope that Maria had brought. 'What is this?' She asked.

'Open it.'

Firdaus ripped off the cover and pulled out the papers from it.

'Are you taking me to court?' She saw the court stamp and assumed it was an appeal for shared custody. 'Are these custody papers?' Her heart sank as she flipped the pages. 'Aryan, I said

I am sorry. Please don't take my daughter away from me. I beg you.'

'Firdaus, I thought you knew how to read.' Aryan smiled.

'What do you mean?' She looked at him in confusion.

'Just read the papers.' He insisted. Firdaus's eyes twinkled out of excitement when she read what was written on it.

'Aryan, this is.' She turned her head to Aryan. He wasn't there. He was down on his knees.

'I don't want to take our daughter away from you. I am here to make a family and not break one.'

'Will you marry me? Asked Aryan.

Firdaus felt her blood rushing to her cheeks, making her blush. She stared at him with her wide eyes, heart still racing and emotions at the cusp of bursting.

'Please give me your answer, my knees are hurting.' He insisted.

'Yes, I will!' Replied Firdaus.

Fact vs Fiction

This story doesn't play around with the history that is already known. It is the unknown part where fiction has met imagination. 'The Lost Necklace' is loosely based on the famous Patiala Necklace that disappeared in 1948. The real story of the Patiala necklace has lots of controversies and enough intrigue to dazzle any history buff. Since the Patiala necklace was never found, and no one knows how it disappeared in the first place, some historical facts have been taken and mixed with fiction to provide closure to the story.

Existence of the Patiala Necklace

The gorgeous Patiala necklace was a one-of-a-kind jewel and a magnificent creation of Cartier Paris. Containing a staggering 2,930 diamonds and weighing over a thousand carats, it was mounted in platinum and enhanced by Burmese rubies. And at its centre were the yellow 234.6-carat De Beers diamond, the size of a golf ball and the seventh-largest diamond in the world. The necklace was made by the finest Parisian craftsmen for Raja Bhupinder Singh of Patiala.

The Patiala necklace sparkled under the light of the Indian sun for two generations, a symbol of power, wealth, and exquisite European taste, but in 1948 it sparked controversy when it was reported missing from the Patiala royal treasury. Nothing was heard of it for a further thirty-four years, till the point when the De Beers diamond mysteriously reappeared, without the necklace, at a 1982 Sotheby's auction (valued at $3 million). Sixteen years after that, parts and fragments of the necklace appeared in a small antique shop in London.

Get to Know the Author

Shaiva Pandya is an accomplished author and versatile content writer, based in Melbourne, Australia. Hailing a master's degree in media and communications from The Parsons University in New York, USA, she channels her creativity as a Web Content Manager at a leading advertising agency in Melbourne.

Her literary journey began in 2017 with the publication of her debut novel, 'Yours Truly, Secret Santa', which garnered acclaim and established her as a noteworthy voice in the literary world. Building on this success, Shaiva recently released her second novel, 'The Lost Necklace', a gripping action-adventure thriller, which she self-published on Amazon. With each work, she continues to captivate readers with her immersive storytelling and imaginative flair.

www.ingramcontent.com/pod-product-compliance
Lightning Source LLC
Chambersburg PA
CBHW020537160726
47991CB00002B/470